BY GRACE DANE MAZUR

The Garden Party

*Hinges: Meditations on the Portals of
the Imagination*

Trespass

Silk

THE GARDEN PARTY

RANDOM HOUSE  NEW YORK

THE

GARDEN

PARTY

∘ A NOVEL ∘

Grace Dane Mazur

██████████

Published in the United States by Random House, an imprint and division of Penguin Random House LLC, New York.

RANDOM HOUSE and the HOUSE colophon are registered trademarks of Penguin Random House LLC.

A small piece of Part One was previously published in very different form, in *Puerto del Sol*.

LIBRARY OF CONGRESS CATALOGING-IN-PUBLICATION DATA
Names: Mazur, Grace Dane, author.
Title: The garden party: a novel / Grace Dane Mazur.
Description: New York: Random House, [2018]
Identifiers: LCCN 2017033805 | ISBN 9780399179723
(hardcover: acid-free paper) | ISBN 9780399179730 (ebook)
Subjects: LCSH: Interpersonal relations—Fiction. |
Families—Fiction. | Domestic fiction.
Classification: LCC PS3563.A9872 G37 2018 | DDC 813/.54—dc23
LC record available at https://lccn.loc.gov/2017033805

Printed in the United States of America on acid-free paper

randomhousebooks.com

2 4 6 8 9 7 5 3 1

Title-page and part-title-page images:
copyright © iStock.com / S-S-S

Book design by Mary A. Wirth

For Barry, Sasha, and Naia

In memoriam

ZEKE MAZUR

1969–2016

CONTENTS

° ° °

∘ SEATING PLAN ∘

PHILIPPA MORRILL BARLOW, 59

Estates and wills

PINDAR COHEN, 60

Beloved

WILLIAM BARLOW, 39

Human Rights? Paris?

LARISSA (Mrs. Barnes Barlow), 35

Studying Japanese?

CHARLOTTE MORRILL (Pippa's Sister), 50-ish

Journalist, society pages

CAMERON BARLOW, 35

Intellectual law

NAOMI COHEN, 24

???

ELIZABETH (Bride!) BARLOW, 28

Large animals. Harry's twin

(Rev.?) HARRY BARLOW, 28

Eliza's twin. What sect is he?

ADAM (Groom!) COHEN, 32

Must be next to Eliza

LEAH COHEN, 91

No elderly dinner partner for her!

OLIVIA (Mrs. William) BARLOW, 33

Very sweet

NATHAN (Pippa's father) MORRILL, 89

Not all there?

BARNES BARLOW, 32

Prosecutor. Terse.

CELIA COHEN, 61

I have no attributes.

SARA COHEN, 29

Scorpions still!

STEPHEN BARLOW, 64

Soon-to-be judge? Lord of golf.

DENNIS LOMBROSO, 37

Sara's Jesuit. Africa.

AMY (Mrs. Cam) BARLOW, 30

I can't seem to get a bead on her.

HARRIET (brilliant) BARLOW, 10

Barnes & Issa's daughter

LIAM (fishes) BARLOW, 7

Cam & Amy's son

ELIOT (mute) BARLOW, 3

William & Olivia's son

EMILY (insects) BARLOW, 8

Cam & Amy's daughter

LAURIE (imperious) BARLOW, 10

William & Olivia's daughter

EMPTY—PROPHET ELIJAH

In case I've forgotten anybody

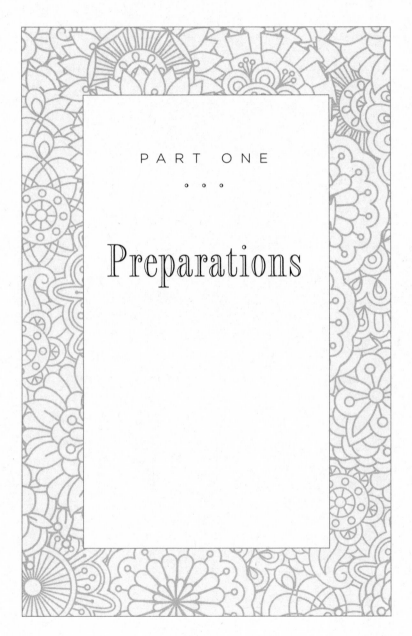

PART ONE

· · ·

Preparations

Near the forest with its small otherworldly pond, the house waits for guests, doors and windows flung open to the warm winds of the summer afternoon. The excitable flower beds toss light and color to one another and toward the weathered shingles of the house, but the brilliance of the sun causes the rooms inside to appear cavernous and dark. Ecstatic chopping noises come from the kitchen, the staccato pulse of knife on wood, scallions mostly, mint. In the main garden, two tables stand end to end, covered with a single long white linen cloth that flutters as though alive, but it is only a passing breeze.

OLD LEAH COHEN sat in the garden while her son, Pindar, lit one last pipe before setting the table. He didn't really have time for a pipe, she thought, but then time had become all jiggery around the edges, like a visual migraine. Today's wedding rehearsal had been at the Barlows' church; it had gone on for an eternity and everyone had been exquisitely cordial but now nothing was ready and all the Barlows would arrive at any moment. Although the two families were not antagonistic, there was an undeniable shyness, a wariness perhaps. Pindar's wife, Celia, came out of the house with a seating plan and a wicker basket.

"What time is it?" their daughter Sara called down from

where she was sitting on the roof. "Are you sure it isn't late?" The house was tall but the slates were not that steep and it was one of Sara's favorite places to sit. It cleared the mind, she said. She had asked earlier if she could help with the tables, but both her parents had said, "Not yet." Though they were used to her being on the roof and didn't worry about her, they could not stop themselves from reminding her every so often to come down.

Pindar checked his list. "And Naomi?"

Celia didn't answer. Shading her eyes from the sun, she called up to the silhouette of her older daughter. "I need you to talk to your sister. Someone's got to get her out of her room."

Sara stayed where she was. "I tried. She said she would think about it, but when I went by a bit later, the door was still locked. She said she was getting dressed."

"When was that?" Celia asked.

"About an hour ago."

Consulting his list, Pindar said, "This African of yours is coming?"

"He's not African," Sara said. "That's where he goes to teach in the summer. And he's not mine. I mean, we're not together."

"But he's coming, right?"

"He'll be here."

"A BIT MORE to your side." Pindar pointed with the stem of his pipe.

Celia tugged the tablecloth smooth. It ruffled again slightly on its own.

"You're not going to surround me with them?" he said.

"That's the point," she replied. "Isn't it?" She lifted the basket of silverware, tarnished and solid, placing it on the table. "Besides, they're hardly strangers. We're about to be related."

"Not until noon tomorrow." He looked at his watch. Not enough time for a nap, barely enough time to get the table done. "They won't stay terribly late, will they?" Raising his face to the sky, he called, "Sara! Where's your sister?"

Sara smiled down at her father. "I just told you. In her room."

"What sort of shape is she in?"

"I'm not sure," Sara said. She knew that although her parents were distraught about her sister, these days—today and tomorrow, at least—were not about Naomi or herself. They belonged to her brother, Adam, and Eliza, his bride. Not only the dinner party and the wedding, but all the currents and eddies of time between and surrounding these events should be theirs. And yet, perhaps because of the odd electric storm in the night, which had done nothing to dissipate the heat or the charge in the atmosphere, perhaps because of her own disastrous phone conversation this morning, time today was darting about, sizzling and unruly, flicking from one person's story to another's.

PINDAR HAD THAT uncanny spatial dislocation of the underslept, as though he were sitting on his own shoulder, stealing puffs from his own pipe. There had been heat lightning and thunder during the night. Although he loved extreme weather, the continual low grumbling in the west had led his dog, Adannu, to panic. Finally he had taken the dog with him into his study, so that Celia could stay asleep. All night long he comforted the dog and did battle with his own thought-demons, who departed shortly before dawn. He slept for an hour or two, then shuffled into the kitchen, still half-asleep, to make breakfast for himself and Celia and bring it back to bed. As usual, he made Turkish coffee in small green cups, plates of toast and jam, and a brass bowl of dates, walnuts, and dried cherries. Today he found some figs, plump as puddings, about to burst their skin; he split a Crenshaw melon and carved it into crescents of pinkish yellow.

In bed, lifting herself on one elbow, Celia had smiled as he set down the tray. "We could, you know, get up," she said. "People do that." Her gray hair billowed. "We could have it down in the kitchen, love. Especially today."

"Can't," Pindar replied. He was not yet out of the vortex of sleep—intense because it had been so brief—and that night wanderer, his soul, might not be able to find its way back if he took his breakfast in an unusual place.

Although Celia did not share his reluctance to go down to the kitchen for breakfast—her soul was always right there, wherever she was, looking out from behind her eyes the minute she opened them—she understood why Pindar liked to bring their breakfast back to bed. Still, she would tease him, saying, "But you were already downstairs grinding the coffee. What if the noise alarmed him and he came home then, your little soul, and didn't find you?"

Pindar said he hoped the errant spindly creature knew enough not to look for him when he was in the kitchen cooking break-fast.

Of course, he didn't always feel such morning fright; there were certain summer mornings when the sky called to him to get his body into the garden. Then he would hurry outside while the early light was still yellow and raking and full of daring.

• • •

THE SOUND OF the wheelbarrow comes from somewhere in the distance, its iron wheel piping like the flutes of the dead.

PINDAR NOW WATCHED Celia counting the plates she had put out. She pointed toward the head of the table to start the count again, as though she was unable to keep track of everyone.

"Twenty-five, my love. You've set for twenty-five."

"Ah. Good."

"But who is the twenty-fifth? By my count we're only twenty-four, including Naomi."

"In case I've forgotten anyone. A straggler, a stranger, Elijah the Prophet."

"So we are setting for Naomi?"

"When I bring my umbrella," Celia began, "it never rains. The laws of protective voodoo positively avert the rain; the same laws of negative preparation would claim that she's more likely to join us if we don't set a place for her . . . but I think we have to do it."

Pindar agreed. That way Naomi would be present even if it was only by the empty place that marked her absence.

"How strange," he said softly. "A whole family of lawyers."

"They're extremely normal. Eliza isn't a lawyer; and what's his name, her twin, also isn't. Here." Celia handed him the forks. "On the left, on top of the napkins," she said.

"On the left?" He always wondered how she knew these things.

Celia knew without being told that he had had an attack in the night, but wasn't sure if it was only the upcoming wedding that was bothering him. She smiled at him and gestured toward the left.

"Do I need a tie?"

"They will all be wearing ties. Except the women. It is, after all, the night before the wedding." Then she corrected herself. "Probably even the women."

"Well then," he said. He was wearing a cobalt-blue dress shirt, a hue so saturated that it was almost not a color but a state of being.

"Actually, dear, knives . . ." Celia tried to say this as though it didn't matter really, as though she weren't even watching, as though it were an afterthought as to which side of the plate the knives went on. She looked up at Sara, whose red hair was now backlit by the sun. Sara, still perched on the slates, caught her mother's glance and shook her head almost imperceptibly, underlining the impossibility of getting her father to set a table in the normal way.

Celia smiled up at her daughter. "You'll be coming down from there, right?"

"Yes. Of course. In a minute," Sara said. She didn't budge.

Sara had acquired the roof habit from her colleagues during a postgraduate year at a biology lab at Oxford. At first she would go with friends but later preferred going solo. Up on those English roofs, shivery and elated, she found she could look down into unsuspecting gardens and discern the crystalline geometry of the clustered houses. It wasn't just the view; the roof was a sort of skin or membrane, pressing against the sky, and like all membranes it was a meeting place of interesting and odd forces. At times, though, up there alone, she would find herself too high; she would wonder, *What on earth?* and then she would freeze, feeling sheets of adrenaline on the soles of her feet, like lightning. *If you move an inch you will slip. You might, in fact, be slipping now.* So she wouldn't move but sat motionless, waiting for the sensation to fade. In stillness she watched the light on the slates of nearby roofs change from pigeon breast through mauve and violet as the walled gardens filled with shadow. Then she would sit some more, in a gargoyle crouch, until, stiff and depleted, wondering if she should feel silly—for her fear, or for the activity itself—she would raise up like a goat unfolding stalky legs and tiptoe back to the open window, where the glass reflected quadrants of deepest blue surrounding the open darkness within.

"I'll put Eliza's mother, Philippa, at this end, the head of the table," Celia called out. "That's how it's done. . . ."

When she didn't continue, Pindar knew that she still wasn't sure where to place everyone. "You won't surround me with them, will you?" he said. Then, smiling as though he had figured out an obscure passage in one of his Babylonian texts, "It's not too late to pull the tables apart, is it? Cohens here; Barlows there. We could call out such friendly toasts. From our table to theirs. Back and forth."

"You're not helping," she said. Her exasperation told him that separate tables had been her first thought, too. They were both feeling shy. "What's eating you?" Celia asked, softly now so Sara wouldn't hear.

Pindar replied, "I'd rather he married an oak tree." He had no idea where that came from. It wasn't really what he meant. Eliza Barlow was a beauty, and their son, Adam, was moon-foolish with love for her. She was studying to be some sort of biologist or veterinarian; she did something with large animals. "Time," he now said, correcting himself. "It will take so much time." He could have been working on his new Babylonian fragments—scraps, really, inscribed in clay with so many parts broken and missing. They had come the previous day from his colleagues in Chicago, and they still had to be pieced together. But no, it wasn't work that he needed. He loved Adam. It was just that this wedding seemed extraneous somehow, and he hadn't been able to enter into the proper festive mood. Sleep was what he yearned for. When everything was over—tonight's gathering and tomorrow's wedding—then perhaps this quivery under-slept feeling would disappear. The Barlows would come and they would go—before midnight, he hoped—and by late tomorrow afternoon he and Celia would be liberated from celebration and they could recapture life as it had been. But what if it ruined things? What if the distance Pindar had recently observed between Adam and his parents only kept growing? What if this marriage proved a disaster for Adam?

Pindar sat down on the smooth rock at the edge of the garden, putting his arms around his knees and his head on his arms. He closed his eyes for a moment or two to get rid of the shakiness that had crept over him. He had been haunted in the night by three words that were clearest on his clay fragment: *layer* (?) . . . *branch* (?) . . . *time*. The question of time had been with him for years—it was the most familiar of his thought-demons—but why did it suddenly feel so catastrophic? Perhaps it was the wedding after all. Which felt like a sundering. Adam was so brilliant and clearheaded. They all depended on their constant conversations with him. But this spring Adam had become opaque. Celia told Pindar that this was normal, that the boy was wrapped up in his own coupling, that his new teaching job at Wellesley had taken all his time. But Pindar couldn't even tell whether Adam was glad to be marrying. It was too late to ask.

• • •

THEY WERE EACH a sort of core for the other, Celia and Pindar: If she was their anchor, he was their bell, their clangor. Their son, Adam, though a poet, was sturdy and calm like Celia; Sara, even now in her early thirties, seemed to spring from nowhere: the sort of abstract puzzle one leaves alone until it explains itself. Perhaps she took after Pindar's mother. And then Naomi, the youngest, always wanting to get away, always needing to be mopped up when she came home, often a bit of a mess. In her, all of her father's sensitivities were still so raw she couldn't deal with them.

In his calmer moments Pindar could feel the turning gears of the heavens. He pictured himself holding hands with Celia and their children and their closest friends, and then the chain would slowly revolve. The problem was, though, all of those people were also gripping others, on out to the edges. What was happening out there at the very margins? Did people spin off into the ether like the tails of galaxies, or the childhood skating game of Crack the Whip? And the other problem, of course, was that at the center of all those streams of people there must be one who turned on his own axis, at the cowlick of the universe. Perhaps he was in the position of that cowlick, licked by some great Babylonian cow-goddess, and thus he himself could appear to stay still while everything streamed around him. At times he would catch himself with the gesture he'd had as a small boy, his right fist turning in a small circle below his motionless left fist, as though he were operating an old-fashioned hand drill, moving the gears of the cosmos. Adam, Sara, and Naomi had always mimicked this gesture as children, giggling as though it were forbidden.

• • •

IN THE MORNINGS, Pindar would work at home on his book about the cooking of ancient Babylon. His recipes were full of gaps, for they had all been inscribed on those fragile tablets of unfired clay.

He was wary of finishing. Celia always had a new book of literary criticism in the works; his son Adam's poetry seemed like an endless river. His daughter Sara had a mind like boxes within boxes, and though all were unmarked he could not conceive of her ever coming to the last box. But Pindar was sure that this book would be his last. He didn't see where he would go after this one. Celia told him not to worry, that things would appear in the cauldron of his mind at the necessary time, but he thought there were no more books in him. She herself complained of too many pots, too many burners. "I am pestered by projects," she would say. "They are all extremely small."

After lunch, Pindar would go in to the university and meet with his students. When his colleagues asked him how his book was going, he tried to seem jolly. "Oh, you know. It's just dreams of eating. Like any other cookbook, only older," he would laugh. "Dabbling in Babylonian stewpots." But he loved his old recipes. In fact, he loved all cookbooks, old or new, perhaps because so few other things in life were such unabashed invitations to delight. When, as a young man, he had invented a sandwich made of peanut butter, bacon, and mango chutney, he thought he might die of pleasure.

WHEN PINDAR AND Celia had discussed the menu for tonight's dinner party he had proposed some of his ancient Babylonian recipes, saying that if one needed something *old* for a wedding, or for the night before the wedding, he had the oldest recipes in the world. "Spiced pigeon pie," he suggested. "Bottéro claims it has a crust of raised dough, though I'm not terribly sure he is correct there. Three thousand five hundred years before Christ, but they must have known better than to raise the crust for a savory pie." He sighed.

"I was thinking we might want something more normal," Celia countered. "After all, we don't know the Barlows very well. We don't know what they like."

"Oh, my family is completely ordinary," Eliza said. "They eat just about anything. What's in your pie?"

"Well, pigeons," Pindar sighed. "We could use chickens, I suppose, though the Mesopotamians didn't have them at the time of this recipe. Eliza, how do your people feel about the alliums?"

Eliza looked at her future father-in-law. "What do you mean?"

"Sorry. It's the onion family. All my recipes have garlic, onions, leeks, shallots, and chives—along with the ever-present cumin and coriander."

"Oh," Eliza said tentatively, as though forcing herself to confess. "My mom claims she's allergic to shallots and onions. But she can eat around them. I don't know how she is with leeks, but scallions are apparently fine. She uses them all the time."

Pindar nodded. Actually he didn't want to make this dish for the Barlows. He had spent years on his translations of the recipe tablets and he cared too much about them to cook them for people he hardly knew. One should never try out a really old dish on strangers.

"Oh Christ," Celia said. "The allergies. I spoke to your mother, Eliza, and she told me everything she could remember on your side of the family." As she hurried off to get her notes, Celia called back to them, "Of course, Naomi claims that eating meat feels like eating one's own grandmother."

Celia reappeared with her journal. "Nathan Morrill—that's Eliza's grandfather, Philippa's father—can't eat ice, ice water gives him hives, and there's something here I can't decipher, about shock and teeth, I think." Hives she didn't want, nor shock, anaphylactic or otherwise. "Yes, and Philippa can't do onions, leeks, or shallots, just as you said. Now, your brother Barnes, he's the prosecuting attorney, yes? No peppers, green or red, and his wife, Larissa"—there was some trouble in that marriage, Celia had heard, one of them was leaving the other, but she didn't know if she was supposed to know, so she wasn't going to mention it—"Larissa is made ill by cloves. Can it be? I've never known cloves to cause anything but numbness. Well, they're easy enough to avoid. No cloves." Celia sipped her coffee. "Now, your brother William, he's the one who lives in Paris? In human rights?"

"Yes. Well. It's only part of the year that he's in Paris, and it's international war crimes, actually," said Eliza.

"I see. Well, I've got here that William is allergic to lemons but not limes, while his wife, Olivia, can't eat wheat, poor creature, no bread, no pasta." Someone was allergic to nuts, one of the Barlow grandchildren, not the three-year-old boy, Eli, though there was something about him—not tragic, Celia had heard, or not yet tragic, but peculiar. Oh God, at three? How did one know at that age if something was tragic or peculiar? Anyway, it was one of the ten-year-old girls who had the thing with nuts, but there were at least a hundred ten-year-old girls in this family, and she had forgotten to note which one. Or was it peanuts? Were peanuts not a real nut, or not a real pea? "Oh God," she said. "If we don't keep track of these things, we could have people seizing up and collapsing all over the place." She wanted the Barlows to be comfortable, she wanted to please them, even. "Ah," she went on. "Next page. Stephen, Eliza's father, doesn't do spicy. Won't touch it. Black pepper is okay, Philippa says, but chilis cause distress. But at least nobody's kosher."

"My family?" said Eliza. "They probably don't know what kosher is."

Celia wasn't sure if Eliza ate mammals; they were, after all, the objects of her vocation. She thought it best not to ask.

"Mutton fat," said Pindar suddenly.

"Dear?"

"You haven't said if anyone's allergic to mutton fat. My recipes are full of the glorious fat from fat-tailed sheep."

"You're not being helpful, my love," Celia said. Then, looking up from her notes, "Pindar! Oh hell. What about your sisters?" Pindar's older sisters had been invited from California. It wasn't clear that they would be able to make it to the rehearsal dinner, but best to be safe. Celia had barely met them. They lived in Orange County and never came east.

"What is it, sweetheart? Those old birds?"

"Exactly. Are they allergic to any foods?" They were appalled, Celia knew, by Pindar's books and his beard and what they thought were unnecessary remnants of Jewishness. They had denied this heritage and sang in the choirs of their adopted Episcopal churches, sent Christmas letters each year tucked inside cards showing snow-filled mangers and turbaned men on camels beneath outlandish stars.

"Oh Lord," Pindar said. "Let me think." He made a muttering *n-n-n-n-na* sound, as though he was spinning through memories of childhood mealtimes. "Althea is allergic to penicillin, and won't eat bread that she suspects of moldiness, or blue cheeses. Thalassa, of course, is allergic to yellow foods. Of any origin. This includes things she thinks might be yellow, such as the sulfites in wine. Gin and vodka, though, having no taint of yellow, are just *nifty*, as she would say. *Swell*. Better buy a case of each."

"Yellow? You can't be allergic to yellow. Not to a color. That makes no sense. Are you sure?"

"She doesn't die. But she vomits. She was projectile as a child. Difficult."

"All right. Okay then. I'll make yellow avoidable." It seemed so hard to keep people happy by feeding them. If they didn't perish, or suffocate, or break out in hives, they threw up. Except for Pindar's mother, Leah, who was so very old. Omnivorous, and stronger than any of them. Leah claimed her heart had turned a bit "quivery," and that her gait had slowed. Still, she walked two miles a day in those peculiarly comfortable black shoes. "How can we cook for all these people without killing them?"

"My darling, we've never achieved the death of anyone before. Listen, find me a cauldron and I can make a Babylonian stew with onions, garlic, and leeks, lamb and mutton fat, and butter, cumin, coriander seed, and cloves. I'll add turmeric, saffron, and preserved lemons just to make it yellow. Then we can make paella with hot pork sausage, chili peppers, and mussels. We will watch everybody keel over, whether they eat from one pot or the other. Food poisoning at a feast goes all the way back: Even Enkidu, companion of Gilgamesh's bosom, died from it."

"Stop it," Celia said, laughing. She hiccuped. "I'll die."

"We could make an enormous cheese soufflé. How is it that none of our friends are allergic to eggs? Surely someone is. Eggs are very propitious for allergies. Leave the cooking to me."

Celia hiccuped again. "No one here is allergic to eggs."

"This is absurd," Pindar said. "This introduction. We haven't met most of your family, Eliza—yet we know all about their innards, their deranged immunities."

Adam and Eliza laughed. Celia wiped her eyes. Pindar shook his head and chewed on his beard; then, self-conscious of appearing to eat himself, he smoothed his beard with his hand.

In the end, of course, he gave up the idea of making dishes that would offend or poison. Cold poached salmon was decided upon, and asparagus and salads and, along with the breads, several batches of corn zephyrs, in honor of Olivia Barlow, who couldn't touch wheat.

PINDAR HAD ALWAYS been a worrier. He thought that this was a reasonable response to his mother, Leah, who never seemed to engage in the fretful sport. He had always felt, even as a young child, that it was up to him to worry for both of them, as his father, Gabriel, had disappeared early on and stayed mostly absent, reappearing only briefly and unannounced, an unpredicted comet. As an adult, Pindar worked at being calm and fluid, but most of the time he was pierced. He was flayed. When he taught in the Near Eastern Studies Department or even when he wrote, his veins ran with quicksilver. Being in the kitchen, cooking, quieted him. Celia calmed him—she was his mooring, his pole driven deep into the earth.

• • •

THERE WAS WORRY, also obsession and anguish; Pindar saved most of his true anguish for his daughter Naomi. This often sent his heart careening, and his longing for Naomi's safety infused many of his quiet moments. But that longing, like most others, could not be uttered, for it would be so easy for the gods to misconstrue it. One could achieve safety in more wrong ways than right ones.

Naomi Cohen had the drive of a visionary without the necessary physical sturdiness. Whenever she returned from one of her missions to try to help others in need, her fair skin would be translucent, her jaw and neck startlingly prominent, her dark eyes too deep-set. Pindar wanted her to be safe and happy but knew that security was not what his daughter was seeking. Over the years he and Celia had rescued her, harbored her, and kept her quiet while she healed. They had plucked her from situations where she was unraveling, always wondering where to place the boundary between altruism and insanity.

In April, Naomi had returned from working in an orphanage outside of Bucharest, where she had gone a couple of years after finishing college. A whole year in Romania had been too long, even she admitted. Pindar feared it would take her almost as long to recover. She had been back for six weeks now and things were still a bit unstable.

On her return from Romania, Naomi had called her parents to ask them to pick her up at the airport. They had been giddy with relief at hearing her voice. Pindar had always felt that there was something fleeting about his daughter, even at twenty-four, as though she were a delicate contraption made of feathers and rubber bands and sails. Instead of landing or anchoring, she seemed only to touch down briefly and intermittently to earth. Whenever he hugged her he feared that she was getting so frail that soon he would not be able to feel her arms around him, feel her cheek against his beard. Celia trusted their daughter a bit more, trusted that she would rebound. Whenever they picked her up from a voyage they were joyous, glowing, and also quiet, so as not to frighten her, not to show how worried they had been and remained. Naomi, however, always seemed wildly happy to see them, whooping and almost dancing. Pindar wondered if he deserved such an abundance. That she should love them both so much, he felt, was a shock, like the cleaving of a crystal.

Logan Airport, the night they went to pick up Naomi, was, as always, full of construction. Pindar disliked construction anywhere, but at airports he felt it was particularly aggressive and wrong. Airports were difficult enough to navigate, and the signage asking the traveler to look for his "terminal letter" always seemed as though he were being asked to reckon the time of his death by figuring out where in the alphabet of existence he would cease. Now Logan had decided to snake all the access roads with curves and buttresses of overpasses that obscured the proper way.

There were no new buildings—anywhere—Pindar felt, that were better than what they replaced; progress always meant the substitution of some new thing that was tacky, expensive, complicated, and unlovable. That all airports everywhere were always under construction was clearly a bad sign, a sign that humans did not know and could not learn how to do things correctly. As airports got bigger one had to wait longer, and thus all travel slowed. Eventually the whole country would be an airport and no one would be able to move.

On that April night Pindar still knew how to find his path through the curving labyrinth, but he wondered about next year's changes, whether loops would arise that would be impossible to exit.

Naomi wasn't outside waiting for them at the international terminal. Even though it was close to midnight, they had expected that she would be right there, sitting on her backpack or standing and waving her arms as though to guide them to a space in front of her.

Inside, the flight monitor did not show any arrivals from Frankfurt. Celia said that Naomi's flight had probably landed so early that it was no longer showing on the board. Naomi also wasn't among those waiting for travelers to appear through the customs doors. Celia checked the café. All around her was the crowing delight of families hugging and reuniting. She wandered the length of the terminal, and then back to the customs barrier again.

Pindar tried to remember if Naomi had mentioned where she would wait for them. He glided up the escalator to the food court, wandered through the domains of oriental-style noodles, tacos, and industrial meat patties, and back again. Finally he noticed someone waving at him and at the same moment he recognized Naomi's posture, the tilt of her head. But her hair had been cropped or shaved—like a convict or a brain patient—and her head was half-covered with a once-red bandanna. It wasn't the shaved head that had kept him from recognizing her, but rather her face. Scratches, sudden and horrible, on her cheeks and forehead made it impossible to look at her squarely. All he could do was glance at her out of the corner of his eye. Only by opening his arms to her, turning his face directly toward her, could he get himself to look. This was a physical effort: He told his body what to do, and it obeyed. He could feel the blood rushing away from his head as panic took its place.

He wanted to save Celia from the sight of her daughter. Perhaps there was some way to clean or cover Naomi's face before he escorted her downstairs. Later he would chastise himself that his first feelings had been to protect himself and Celia from having to gaze on her.

"My Naomi." He bent down to kiss her. "We couldn't find you." She stood up to hug him and he held on to her, rocking her gently but not wanting to take her wind away. She was slighter than ever. It was like hugging a moth.

The girl gave Pindar such a lopsided smile that he wondered if she had had a stroke or some sort of palsy, something to do with a facial nerve. He would have to look it up.

"Dad," Naomi said. "I thought you'd never get here."

Pindar looked around for her luggage, but all he could see was a small leather document purse and a bottle of spring water.

"Oh," she said. "My stuff. It's over there behind the chair. I'm afraid it sort of got scattered." She bent down to stow a toilet kit and a sweater in her knapsack. "I got in a while ago, actually. I wanted to decompress a bit before I called you."

"Have you eaten?" He meant *Have you eaten since you left home a year ago?* She looked inside out, she was so thin. She looked like a compound fracture.

"Not too much," she said. "I was waiting till I got home to you and Mom. With all the travel, my stomach's been a bit off." She handed Pindar a stack of newspapers, saying sheepishly, "I guess I should get rid of these. Do you want to dump them for me?"

Pindar saw, as he carried the papers to the trash bin, that they were not foreign, as he had supposed, but were the past three days' editions of *The Boston Globe*. Had she found them discarded somewhere? Or was it, and he hated to think that this was more likely, that she had been living in the airport for days? He gulped back tears. He didn't dare ask her how long she had been there or where she had slept, or why she had delayed so long to call home.

Pindar heaved the knapsack onto his back. As they rode the escalator he reached down to touch his daughter's shoulder, barely feathering it. At street level, she ran to Celia and hugged her, both women caught by the joy and strangeness of reunion. In the car, Naomi climbed into the back and asked if it was okay if she took a bit of a nap. She lay down, and Pindar could see in the rearview mirror that she was soon fast asleep.

He whispered to Celia, "What on earth do you think—"

"Shh," Celia interrupted, putting a finger to her lips. "Later."

THE NEXT MORNING found Naomi in the local supermarket. It was early still and everyone had been asleep when she left the house. Generally she hated supermarkets, but she thought that today this one could, if not cure her, give her system a much-needed nudge back to normal, simply by her rolling a shopping cart up and down the adamantly bright aisles.

In the produce section she stopped to inhale the smell of so many oranges—Valencia, blood, juice, navel—net bags of limes, stacks of pineapples. The hygienic overtones of bleach were also in the air and she sniffed at the scent of chlorine as though it were a delicacy. She picked up a watermelon as big as a child, lifting it with difficulty into her cart. A sheaf of plantains. Peaches thick with fuzz.

She chose bottled waters from Maine and Italy, from Germany and France, then proud-colored squeeze bottles of Joy and Cheer, Dove and Palmolive. She reached for high-protein cereals and protein bars, granola with cranberries, Cap'n Crunch. She explored the store, lapping up the light, listening to the music with its brave half-heard songs of love lost and found.

Naomi passed by the stacks of mammalian flesh cut into portions wrapped in tight plastic. She lingered at the fish counter to contemplate the blackness of the mussels, the glistening dislocated stripes of the mackerel, the rosy pinkness of the salmon fillets arrayed on the ice. Here were animals still with their eyes on, red snapper and Mediterranean black bass. In a tank of greenish water, lobsters swam with halting deliberation; she pursed her lips and gave a furtive salute, her fingers held like claws.

When her grocery cart got full, Naomi made her way back through the store. Slowly, purposively, every so often she returned something to the shelf where it belonged. In this manner, shopping and un-shopping almost equally, she kept her cart a little over half-full. By always seeming to be doing exactly what the other shoppers were doing she drew no attention to herself, even when she had been there most of the morning.

Toward the end of this time, Pindar was also in the supermarket, watching his daughter's strange method of perpetual shopping. He had found her note on the kitchen table, saying that she was going for a walk and then to the market to pick up a few things.

When he spotted her in the store, he went back to the entrance and got an empty carriage, as this would allow him to observe and follow her without seeming like a stalker.

Wheeling his carriage through the store, Pindar couldn't think of what to shop for; it was impossible to remember anything that he needed or wanted. Finally he took a couple of bottles of spring water in order not to seem like some crazy guy with an empty carriage and a head full of panic. It was expensive water, in dark blue bottles. But that tiny load seemed unnaturally Spartan, so he added an onion, a single can of tuna fish. Now he looked divorced. Or widowed. This terrified him. All he wanted was a certain consuming camouflage so that he could keep an eye on his daughter.

In the cereal aisle, Pindar watched as Naomi put a box of Froot Loops back on the shelf. Keeping a fair distance, he followed her to the soaps, where she returned the Palmolive dish detergent and the Cascade, taking a box of S.O.S scouring pads in exchange. She was absorbed, not in her shopping but in something more inner, and she did not see her father as he slowly trailed her through the store. He wondered if her mood was ending now, as her carriage was getting emptier. She looked as though she was gathering herself up for something, preparing to give or receive.

When Naomi had at last unburdened her carriage of all but a box of dark chocolates with an elephant on the cover, Pindar came up behind her and gently tapped her arm.

She turned to him. "Dad." She smiled. "Land of plenty." She swept her arm to indicate the well-stocked shelves. She seemed stronger after a night's sleep. Her face, still covered with open scratches, showed no signs of healing.

"Sweetie. Shall I take you home? Have you got what you need?"

Naomi had gotten what she needed, actually, though she didn't know how to explain to her father that what she had wanted was to be submersed in the bounty that is the American supermarket, a place she normally avoided. The impersonality, the anonymity, the luscious and disgusting excess—this was the way she had learned over the years to relocate herself after harrowing travels: to wander under the canned music facing the onslaught of the possible, fingering the redundancies of choice until she could stop listening to what was bothering her, in this case the sad smell of the hopeless babies in the Romanian orphanage. Instead, she remembered the boy in the countryside, walking his bony cow at the end of a rope, and the gentle way he asked her if she wanted to buy the cow's bell.

"Is it time to go?" Naomi asked.

"It's noon," Pindar said. "Celia's making lunch for us. Is there anything you crave?"

"Nothing," she said, shaking her head. "Everything," she clarified, smiling.

"Those chocolates?"

"Could you? I don't have a cent on me."

Later, after Pindar had driven Naomi home and she had gone upstairs, he and Celia stood in the kitchen beside the coffee machine, whose hissing sounds they were ignoring.

"Easily a couple of hours," Pindar said. "Taking things down and putting them back." He explained how Naomi hadn't reshelved items she had just taken, but the things at the bottom of the carriage, which she had taken earlier.

"Did she put them in the right places?"

"As far as I could make out. Is that a good sign?" He paused then added, "It wasn't that she was caressing the objects, but she could have been. What do we do? Do we ask her about it? What do we do about her face?"

"Do we know anyone who does tropical medicine?" Celia asked.

"It was Eastern Europe, my love, not the tropics."

"I know. But it looks so raw and burning, her face. And she looks so thin. What if it's leprosy? Do you think it's leprosy?"

Celia called her own doctor and was terrified when she got an appointment for Naomi that same afternoon.

It wasn't leprosy. Or not real leprosy, though that might show up in the future. It seemed to be a strep infection, from being scratched by babies at the orphanage. Naomi came home from the doctor with antibiotics, a regimen of vitamins and food. If she ate properly, the doctor predicted, her face would be healed in a month or six weeks, in time for her brother's wedding in June. Or at least healed enough for makeup.

That evening, after dinner, curled up in the corner of the living room couch, Naomi told her parents that she had, in fact, spent three days and nights in Logan Airport before calling them, needing, she said, some halfway atmosphere, someplace that was neither here nor there. She had not been the only inhabitant, she said. Each night she saw a dozen others, some with bags, some without, most of them as friendly and wary as she was. She slept one night on a pew in the chapel, part of another night in the handicapped stall of one of the women's restrooms in Terminal B. Most of the seats in the waiting areas had armrests—to keep people like herself from stretching out—but there were some where the armrests could be folded out of the way. If anyone asked her what she was doing, she simply said her evening flight had been canceled and she was waiting to fly out the next morning. It wasn't that she didn't want to go home to her parents, she told them, it wasn't that at all. Rather, it was that she thought she might break apart at the difference between the squalor of the orphanage and the cozy beauty of home. When the airport finally began to feel alien, she said, and when she noticed how acrid and gray and tasting of burnt kerosene the air was, then she knew it was time to pack up her things, time to go back home.

• • •

PLACING BRASS VASES of flowers along the midline of the set table in the garden, Pindar called out, "Celia! I have a sexual imbalance here."

"Not now, darling. Now is not the moment."

"No, no. On the table. I have black-eyed Susan, goatsbeard, and some early Queen Anne's lace. We need another man. Do you think bachelor's button would do? Is the jimsonweed in bloom?"

Celia saw the implications of choosing either a traditional bachelor's flower or a fatally toxic, if lovely, member of the nightshade family. Walking over from the drinks table, she said, "You are a mischief and a nasty old goat. Pull yourself together. Besides, the Jimson of jimsonweed was not a man, it is a contraction of the word Jamestown." She gave him a kiss. "I know you can find something."

Pindar considered the two standing candelabras, which he had carried out from the dining room. It was too early to light the candles, but when else would he have a moment? He lit them and rekindled his pipe; he sucked on it sharply, then exhaled, surrounding himself with smoke. Up on the roof his daughter Sara was waving to him. Golden girl. Only she could crouch that way, utterly comfortable with her knees up to her ears, for hours at a time. Whenever she was up there she looked as though some joint or ligament had been put on backward. Perhaps it came from consorting with scorpions.

SARA *HAD* SPENT a lot of time with scorpions, though mostly in the abstract—that is, they were mostly dissected. As a biologist she had looked at how they grew and shed their skins, their cuticles. This was the wonderful ancient problem of any animal whose skin was also its skeleton: how to grow larger when you were covered with a solid coat of armor that could not grow. The solution for scorpions was the same as for insects, crabs, lobsters, and their kin. The answer, of course, lay in folding. The trick was to grow an intricately folded soft new skin just inside the old one, then to break and burst through that old armor, and finally to expand and smooth out the new covering, later hardening it. Many of the scorpions, when their new skin was hard enough, would glow with a brilliant blue or green fluorescence under ultraviolet light. The evolutionary advantage this might confer was not yet known, but it did make them easy to find in your room at night, if you had the right sort of flash-light.

Sara had loved this uncanny glowing of the scorpions, and much of her research involved studying their fluorescence. Their strange flexibility she found frightening but also captivating. Every move seemed part of a ritual dance.

Perhaps it was her Jesuit friend Dennis's fault that soon after she got her doctorate she left the laboratory, left biology alto-gether. "Misspent was my youth," she wrote him. "So horribly. Not to have read Milton, Chaucer, Ovid, or anyone else, versed only in the autistic jargon of science. Every night and afternoon in the lab, also every noon and morning, pouring toxic liquids back and forth. Hoping for flashes of beauty."

The life of the scorpion—or of any other being—must be more, she thought, than the little gears and cogwheels of mech-anisms that allowed it to happen. She felt that the mechanisms were preventing her from seeing the animal in itself, the True Scorpion. For too long she had been looking at the animal as an endpoint of processes, biology explained by chemistry explained by physics—the ever-smaller effects and causes embedded in one another like Russian dolls until some last tiny quarklike nubbin was all that could be imagined.

Sara knew other biologists found "beauty" in scientific explanations, but to her this was just beauty by analogy. Real beauty could be perceived only by the senses, never the intellect. What the intellect could see was only "as if." When her friends exulted about the beauty in science or in a mathematical proof, they meant a sparseness, "economy" they called it, ideas pared down to the leanest, most miserly utilitarian form. But such a Spartan lack of ornamentation, such meanness, was almost never found in the beauty of the natural world. The beauty of nature, she felt, contained a generosity of uselessness. Unnecessary decoration, a wondrous too-muchness. When Sara recognized that thinking like this meant she was a lousy scientist, she saw that it was time to get away from the lab, to get away from killing things and breaking them down in order to see how they worked. It was time to pay attention to people, their stories, their ideas.

For a while she strutted about the laboratory with the clarity of her resolve to quit. Unable, though, to completely let go of the scorpions, she had written a piece for a popular science magazine about scorpions in the ancient world. Too soon, it seemed as though she were an authority on the topic. She wasn't any sort of expert; it was just that few other people were writing on the subject. In any case, now she was out of the lab and had received a fellowship to write on scorpions in present-day folklore.

• • •

CELIA TOUCHED THE flapping tablecloth to quiet it. She liked having the long table out in the garden; its dislocated formality was inviting and puzzling. This pleased her, as did the way the cloth seemed to heave on its own every so often. But still some bother twinged; it had been insinuating itself all week into the spaces of her mind, darkening the edges of even the sweetest thoughts.

Celia, too, felt that their son, Adam, had become veiled with the approach of his wedding to Eliza. She thought this was probably as it should be. Couples on the eve of their wedding turn inward, she knew this, but she was sad that he had stopped sending his poems to Pindar and herself. She hoped it was because he was writing privately to Eliza, but she was not sure.

At sixty-one Celia Cohen found herself suddenly at the age when if she greeted friends only slightly older, she would find their skeletons grinning back at her. *What,* she would think, *so soon?* And she would wonder how much she had in common with those bony, blear-eyed faces. Her shoulders were rounded from years of joyful hunching over books, and she feared decay and breakage as well as her tendency toward all-over roundness, which led her to perform calisthenics every morning. If the day was fine she would also go into the woods and practice some once martial, but for her peaceful, art.

For the past year Celia had felt the need to test her memory, so she set herself the task of learning two lines of a poem every day. Of course she lost her keys, her glasses, but this seemed as much a part of the aging process as graying hair. She was not at all concerned with memory of things and where they hid themselves. It was memory of the written word she was after. She wondered if she was also forgetting two old lines a day. Or perhaps more. Was the outflow greater than the inflow? Or was it just a slow leak? She checked for brain failure due to age or tumors by examining all the senses: Could she still find wild strawberries in the woods? Could she tell one salvia from another by the feel of the fuzz on its leaves? Or taste the difference between a blackberry and a black raspberry? Could she still determine where an old book had been published by the smell of its ink? During the day her garden-calloused fingers would try to feel the wood grain of her desk, underneath all the papers stacked there. She would test herself in other ways, too, trying to see if she could remember the faces of students who wrote asking for letters of recommendation. This last was the hardest.

Whenever she could take the time from the English department, Celia would garden. At first she would resist, but then once she was down and dirty, perhaps because of the oxygen coming from the plants themselves, perhaps because she was dealing with the fecundity of the underworld and all its roots and thus the etymology of bloom, perhaps because it made her look forward with such radiant hope—she didn't know what it was, but once she had started digging and planting she could not get herself to go back to the house until the light was gone. Most of the time she saw her garden as shaggy with wanting, weeds overgrown with their own delight. Occasionally, though, small corners of terrain or even single plants seemed to approach some ethereal ideal, as when one day a friend had left on her front porch an immense dahlia of impossible color, a sort of smoky rose gold, aureate.

It wasn't that Celia didn't like dinner parties; she loved them. The emotional fields hovering among the guests—these stood out for her like strands of colored smoke. Not only the erotic forces, but all the other psychic currents she saw as neon strands of cat's cradles, glowing as though they were external neurons, which—if one paid enough attention—one could untangle and weave into a narrative of the emotions. It was easy to do this about other people, especially strangers, but so hard to unravel the strands of oneself.

She loved parties, but she felt insufficient with all those lawyers coming to her house, inspecting. The floors were clean, everything glowed, but she didn't know what they would be expecting. Did this mean they would now come over for Thanksgiving? And would she have to go to their Christmas festivities?

She would be correct to Philippa and Stephen, but she didn't want to be implicated. Just because the young couple had connected, that was no reason for their parents to zipper up, one tribe to the other, and so on back through the generations. Such zippering, such sudden relatedness, was too abrupt. She knew that her thoughts were venomous and mean-spirited and that probably the Barlows didn't want this zippering any more than she did. Yes, some sort of marriage ceremony needed to be invented where such mixing was stopped, a kidnapping, say, followed by a single joining, with no spread or seepage back through the older generations. She saw that she was championing the idea of elopement.

SARA HADN'T REALLY told her parents much about her friend Dennis; nor had she talked of him to Naomi. But she had finally mentioned him to her brother a few weeks earlier. "Wait a bloody minute!" Adam had said. "You've been with this guy for a year and none of us have even glimpsed him? What's going on? Is he married?"

"Nope."

"What's wrong with him?"

"Nothing at all. I'm mad about him."

"You've got to bring him, then. This means a lot to me. Will he come?"

"Do you mean to the dinner or the wedding?"

"Both."

"I'll ask."

SARA'S FRIEND DENNIS Lombroso wasn't married. He was a Jesuit priest. For a year she had been making clandestine visits to him in his cottage in Newton at the girls' school where he lived and served as chaplain. She would drive her red Toyota across the river late at night and park under the old oak trees by the stone wall. Trying not to look furtive she would unlock the iron gate, whose rusted hinges she oiled from time to time. Then she would hurry through the chaplain's garden with its disheveled roses and slip in through the kitchen door.

Early in the morning she would glide away, dressed but unshowered, still smelling of sex. Driving home to her apartment in Somerville just over the Cambridge line, she would wonder how many of those schoolgirls were sweet on young Father Dennis, with his Mediterranean skin, his green eyes, his clipped black beard.

She hadn't intended to fall in love with a priest. Not seriously. In the early days of their friendship, with its exhilarating and argumentative chatter, Dennis claimed that it was only talk that he was after. "I'm not courting you, you know."

"I know that," Sara said. "You're a priest." Dennis was the purest person she had ever met. She was fascinated by his disregard for her charms; the more he seemed immune, the more she could not stop herself from trolling for his desire.

"I've never talked with a Jewish woman," Dennis said one day. They were eating lunch in Cambridge, in a cellar café with yellow walls.

"And how do you find us?" Before he could answer she added, "Actually, I'm not sure I'm representative."

"Do you think I am?" he countered. "Representative, I mean. Do you suppose *we're* all the same?"

"Of course not," Sara said. "But my Jewish friends complain that my particular religious sect is not even Jewish: 'Too many gods,' they say, 'and only one adherent.'"

Sara's book group was reading Ezekiel—wheels and eyes and flames, lapis lazuli and gold, likenesses and appearances. The group, all women, mostly Jewish, found her lovable but suspected that she was hallucinatory, for she claimed she saw gods everywhere: She said she was often "bumping up against the divine." Her friends didn't really know what to make of it. Though of Jewish descent, she seemed to them like some nondenominational mystic, some sort of rogue or ronin, who, through no virtue of her own, was born with a particular sensitivity, the way others might show from earliest childhood musical or mathematical brilliance.

Explaining herself to Dennis, Sara told him that in contrast to his god or the god of the Hebrews, all of her deities were stunningly minor: God of the Doorknob, she confessed, God of the Hinge, God of the Ball Bearing or the Missing Jacket Button.

"Oh," he said. "Now I can place you. The ancient Romans had a goddess of the hinge, named Cardea. Forculus was their god of the doorpost, and Limentinus the god of the threshold. I don't know if they had gods of the doorknob or the missing button, but they had so many small household deities that they could have. How does it feel to be an ancient Roman?"

Sara smiled. "It makes the world sort of . . . glow."

How had Sara reconciled such consorting and holy mischief with her work as a research biologist? For one thing, she would never mention these small gods to her scientific colleagues. For another, the bio labs at Harvard were full of closet theists of one kind or another. Some gave public sermons at the morning prayers in the chapel of Memorial Church. Others invoked the notion of "non-overlapping magisteria." Sara belonged to neither camp.

Perhaps because of her odd connections with the divine, Sara was drawn to people who were ordained in the normal religions. Sometimes she would work in the Divinity School library, and take her meals in what she called the Divine Café. Perhaps, when she first encountered Dennis Lombroso there, she had, on some unconscious level, been hunting for holy men.

Dennis had not been hunting for anyone. After his studies at Boston College and Loyola, he was simply taking a class in anthropology at Harvard at night, to help him with some of his summer projects in Africa.

Finally Dennis started to telephone Sara in the evenings. She pretended to be unaware but she could feel the heat rising. When they met for coffee in Cambridge he brought her things from his garden: tulips wrapped in newspaper, bunches of green coriander and thyme. She could foretell how their story would go and was anxious about his eventual fall. All the gods in the world, large or small, were no match for the human heart.

• • •

Sara had spent the night before the garden party at her parents' house. It had been a rattled night. Whenever the storm was quiet the cries of forest animals would cut through the darkness, one pair right below her window sounding like a snake fighting with a teakettle. When finally she slept she dreamed she was a very tall plant; she didn't fit completely in the bed, something to do with her roots or her fronds.

Now, up on the roof, Sara was surveying everything, starting with her mother's garden spread out below her. Normally there would be a sweet primness on this first day of June, but because of the unusually warm weather it was displaying all the erotic wildness of late July, raucous in parts, lush and green. She took in several deep breaths. She wasn't sure what her family would make of Dennis. She herself didn't know what to make of him: In between moments of deciding she should leave him, she longed for him. He was at the other end of each of her thoughts. Pluck any strand in the universe and it would be made of the threads that linked him to her. Within minutes he would be here at the house. This made time quiver with aboutness.

They had both known their relationship was to be without future, offspring, or consequence. The one time she had dared ask Dennis about their future he had told her that the only way he could see himself leaving the Church was feet first. Perhaps they would break up tonight. She shouldn't have invited him, didn't know why she had listened to her brother, Adam. Maybe it was time that the whole thing ended.

Dennis's messages from the past few days now seemed dark and full of portents. Early this morning Sara had phoned him knowing that his voice would soothe her after the turbulence of the night. Which it did, except that just before he hung up he happened to utter that hackneyed phrase so full of menace, "We have to talk." She knew that this phrase was anti-performative: It always meant there would be *no* more talking, *no* more of the whispers and exultations of lovers.

"We are talking," she replied, stunned. "Hi."

"You know what I mean," Dennis said. "Face-to-face."

"Oh," she said. She looked at the phone as though she were holding a small animal with vicious teeth, not quite dead. She dropped it onto her bed without hanging up and left the room. Dennis had beaten her to the breakup. Had it been a race, then?

"NOT BESIDE STRANGERS," Pindar murmured.

But Celia had left the garden.

BORSUK THE GARDENER was carrying chairs from the dining room to the long table in the garden. "Last up from the table in this world," he called out to Chhaya, the cook, "first at the banquet in the next." As he positioned the chairs, he thought of how they would ruin the lawn by the end of the party. Luckily last night's electrical storm had brought no rain with it. He went to the garage and loaded folding chairs into his wheelbarrow. Mrs. Celia had borrowed them from her university.

Borsuk's history varied each time it was told, and the Cohens had given up trying to piece together the man's true story. He was Polish; that much seemed sure. Perhaps he really was, as he sometimes claimed, a distant relative of Celia's family. When Pindar had first met him, while at a conference in Poland, Borsuk had been the curator of a small museum in Krakow, but he soon lost favor with the Communist authorities. Then came difficult times, he said, after which he had worked as a waiter and finally had no job at all. Now that Pindar and Celia had sponsored him to come to the States, he worked as their gardener and he said that he was as close to being happy as he could imagine. He lived in an apartment over the garage, where he filled his notebooks with Polish writings in the evenings. When they asked him what he was writing about, he would smile and say, "Just writings. You know. Just things." When they asked about his family he shook his head and murmured, "Gone."

LEAH COHEN WALKED in the garden that had once been hers and now belonged to her son, Pindar, and his wife. The long table was finally all set for the dinner party. Under the birch trees she saw Celia talking to young Eliza, who was in tears. The girl stood on the grass in her lime-green socks, and something about the way she stood pierced the old woman and made her blush.

Leah, at ninety-one, felt that she had not changed much in the past decade. Her knees worked sweetly, if a bit slowly, as did her hips. Her fingers were agile and she could knit or sew if she wanted, which she didn't. With the years her face had lengthened, but she was pleased that her ears had remained small, not turning into the flaps that had appeared on some of her friends. Her nose had always been a mighty thing; now it was like the beak of an eagle. Her lips were as full and dark as ever, though her mane, which she still wore loosely on top of her head, was almost pure white.

When she had been in her forties Leah had hoped to become thin as a lily stalk, so thin and light that she could swerve out of the path of the darts that the gods were so fond of flinging down. During the next half century she never achieved slightness; instead she turned columnar, like an old oak, a bit oxlike through the middle but tall and unstooped. Long walks each day were what kept her old bones alive. She wore running shoes even today, with her long purple dress. They were made of black leather and no one was allowed to notice them.

Stopping beside the hollyhocks, Leah paused. *Heavens!* she thought. *Life! The world is swirling with possibilities, a universe of things that we can touch with our infinite fingertips, see!* She felt as though she were inside the cat's-eye marble that she had wrapped up to give to Adam as a wedding present. *Look! Put your fingers out in the air, like this. Feel it? Feel the swirling? Sometimes we can condense them like mist, the possibilities, and hold them in cupped hands. Here, catch!* But who was she silently talking to? She turned back to gaze at the two women, Celia comforting Eliza.

Leah couldn't place the appearance of the weeping girl's bare arms and stocking feet, or the feeling they awoke in her. As old as the century, her world was populated by visions—echoes of old configurations—and she was bewildered and embarrassed when she could not connect these echoes with a definite time and place. She felt now as though she had seen this young bride somewhere else, in the buoyant light of some earlier summer. Was it in Oxford, where Leah had grown up? Or later, in Paris, between the wars? Watching Eliza talk to Celia, Leah had that sharp intake of breath that comes when one forgets to guard against desire, when the heart itself seems to gasp for air.

"What was I thinking?" Eliza groaned to her future mother-in-law. She had drunk too much for early afternoon.

"Ah," replied Celia.

Eliza put her forehead against the tree. "Why didn't you force us to elope?" she asked. "My mother has had fits all morning—about the dress, about my refusing to have any bridesmaids. Good Lord. Bridesmaids."

"Well, exactly," Celia said, trying to appear nonjudgmental. Which was hard, for she had, in fact, begged Adam and Eliza to run off without telling her, if they insisted on marriage. Do it all privately, my loves, she had told them. Do it somewhere else. You will be so much happier.

"She makes it all loom so," Eliza went on. "She thinks it's *her* drama. She knows I'm allergic to all her roses. But she burst into tears at the bouquet I made: alfalfa, clover, timothy, and corn. Oh look, another bat. Man's dusk is bat's dawning. It's much too early for bats. It's nowhere near dusk. What is that little guy doing?"

A car door slammed in the distance. Eliza flinched.

"Dearest," said Celia. "Be quick. Get yourself away and steal some minutes alone. Go up to the pond. I'll deal with your parents, everyone." She reached up and brushed Eliza's pale hair back from her face, then stepped back and looked at the pretty girl in her cranberry-colored dress. "You can't go there in socks. Don't you want some shoes?"

Eliza shook her head. She pulled off one green sock at a time, stuffing them into her small beaded purse, which had been given to her by her mother for this occasion. Then she hugged the bosomy Celia, mother of the man she loved and keeper of this strange household with all its sweet nights, its unfamiliar words and mysteries and interesting messes.

• • •

WITH HIS HANDS in his pockets, Pindar ambled in the direction of the stone wall, trailing smoke. The Solomon's seal, which should have been in bloom, had already gone by. He would use Jacob's ladder, then. It was ahead of itself. The whole summer was ahead of itself, with the full heat of August on this first day of June. Voices drifted in from the driveway. Barlows. What did they all talk about at home, around the dinner table? *Point of order, point of order?* Eliza's father, Stephen Barlow, looked like someone waiting for a judgeship. He looked as though he always had a gavel hidden behind his back. *Toc toc.* Would he bring the gavel to the dinner table, along with a stack of thick books with identical bindings, to search for precedents? *Toc toc. Turnips overruled. Where's my soup?*

At their first meeting, Stephen Barlow had asked Pindar if there was something wrong with Adam that he had become a poet—implying that poetry was not a calling but a failure of will or a malady of the soul. Laughing to mask the earnestness of his question, Barlow asked, "Was he . . . troubled as a child?" He was full of visible concern, as though discussing some obscure neurological syndrome with embarrassing symptoms. Pindar saw that poems, with their telegraphic electricity, their iridescent ambiguity, seemed to Stephen Barlow like ghosts of eels, shadows of bubbles. Pindar had not been able to reply to the question about Adam's childhood. Instead he had stood there, sucking his pipe, silent as a stroke victim, staring straight ahead until Celia darted over to save him, breaking into their stalled conversation. Celia often kept her antennae tuned to Pindar's talk as well as her own.

How could Eliza in her wine-colored dress and light green socks have sprung from the Barlow clan? Pindar wondered.

Surely she had been adopted. But then, what about her twin, Harry, with his angular cheekbones and those blue-black ringlets? He seemed like a sweet boy. Perhaps both Eliza and Harry had been changelings, and a pair of infant lawyers, twins, had ended up residing in a different family altogether.

By the wall Pindar opened his penknife and cut several stalks of Jacob's ladder. He liked the thought of Harry Barlow as minister. If one had to get married, and if the ceremony had to be Christian, which the Barlows took for granted though Pindar preferred the canopy and smashed wineglass of his own tribe, then someone who had been defrocked the way Harry Barlow had was just the thing. Not defrocked exactly, but expelled from seminary. Pindar sucked sharply on his pipe, then exhaled, surrounding himself with smoke. Harry Barlow had broken into the caged book section of the Divinity School library late one night. It wasn't clear what he'd been looking for, but he didn't find it, only art books containing nudes. Not even pornography. No ideas, simply bodies. What a fuss the librarians had made when they found him lying there in the morning, asleep among the naked art. But what kind of a school would still keep books in a cage? Harry was well out of it.

Of course the boy had some sort of license now. It would all be perfectly legal. Old Judge Thick-Books would have seen to that.

THE DOME OF coolness above the pond throbs with croaking. Dragonflies and damselflies pierce the slanting light that burnishes the surface of the water with fire. At the edges frogs wait to spring.

• • •

ELIZA HELD THE skirt of her dress as she stepped into the water. Instead of heaving and railing she ought to be thinking. Consider, for example, the ostrich and the emu; were they, metabolically speaking, more like horses than birds? There was so much she didn't know. She was still surprised that she had gotten into vet school for the coming fall semester. She would commute from Wellesley to North Grafton. Yesterday she had been wondering about deer and their antlers: Somebody must understand, but she did not, how the antlers knew, each successive year, that they must grow more points or branches than the previous year, the old pair having been shed after the rutting season. Was it some sort of hormone, which didn't get broken down but just accumulated season after season in the maturing stag? All she knew about antlers was that the blood supply was in the velvet. It was said that squirrels ate fallen antlers for the calcium and other minerals. That was why you didn't find them all over the place in these Brookline woods. Probably tasted a little salty, crunchy like the bones of quail. Perhaps she should get her mother to serve platters of thin-sliced antlers at the wedding lunch tomorrow, as hors d'oeuvres. If antlers were nutritious, perhaps horn was beneficial after all, rhinoceros horn, for example. Except that horn was keratin—like toenails, not bone—like skull. But first came tomorrow. Tomorrow she would be parading under her mother's arbor, exhibiting Adam to her parents' friends, making their private intimacies public, trying not to sneeze.

Pindar's dog came back from hunting squirrels in the woods and barked at Eliza: Up to your knees in the water? Want company? Any fish?

"You stay there," Eliza said. "I'll be right out."

The animal sat, ardent, waiting.

FROM THE ROOF Sara watched Dennis walk into the garden. She knew this evening was not hers, that she should not be thinking about herself. Nothing would get resolved; she wanted to weep—for the complexity and the impossibility of it all. It was sad craziness, her love for this man. Everything felt unsafe, even her place on the roof. In spite of everything, she shuddered with desire at seeing him down there below her, unaware that she was watching him. She had to put her hands down for balance. The hard sun-warmed slates grounded her but she was still so high that her heart kept pounding. She wanted to call out to him but decided to keep silent to prolong the moment—that state of in-betweenness before everything else had to commence.

Dennis was wearing a light-colored suit that Sara had never seen. He carried a small wrapped package. As he went along the path he stopped to look at the plants. He paused by the kitchen plot to pick leaves from the aromatic herbs and rub them in his hands. He lingered among the flower beds, bending to smell or to touch the petals. When he got to the statue hidden by the yew bushes he laughed, then backed off to see it from a bit farther away. He shifted his head from side to side, then, imitating the figure, he lifted his hands to play an imaginary flute and raised one knee in a Bacchic dance.

When Celia heard Dennis laughing near the statue she came to greet him and introduce herself.

"Oh, you caught me dancing with this faun fellow! I am so glad to finally meet you," he said. "Your plume poppies are glorious," he said. "The whole garden is. I hope you will walk me through it when there's time."

"Of course I will." Celia almost hugged him for his appreciation. "I'm so glad you like the poppies. I can give you some if you like, but they are complete thugs. Hooligans! They escape wherever you put them, they multiply and take over. You really have to keep an eye on them."

"I can do that," Dennis said. "I would love some."

HEARING ADANNU BARKING in the distance, Adam Cohen looked out the window of his room. He had showered and shaved and combed his hair, which seemed a darker red in its wetness. Tall, skinny, and naked, he had put on his wire-rimmed glasses but hadn't yet found anything else to go with them. He wondered how to describe the light of the candles his father had lit—not yellow, not white, barely visible gleams in the late sun of the garden. The candles stood on holders like bound sheaves of harpoons, made by a friend who was a blacksmith. Adam had not yet written about working metal, firing it red-hot, white, the fire inside the forge, the forging inside the fire, the hammering, tempering, quenching, twisting—the clangor and hiss of the black iron, smithed among the ringing gerunds. He longed for a couple of hours alone in his room with yellow pad (faint lemon) and yellow pencil (school bus). A fit of sudden shyness and sleepiness. He had spent the night here in his childhood room and had kept waking with the thunder, unable to place himself. He wished he had a more solid footing for this day. Why did people throw rice at weddings? Why not pearls? Vowels and consonants?

Down below, his mother carried a ceramic pitcher of water to the wooden table, then went over to the stone wall and said something in Pindar's ear. Pindar leaned toward her to ask her something then rubbed his beard on her cheek.

Coming back toward the house, Celia noticed Adam standing at his window, still not dressed, or only half-dressed. "Hey," she called softly. "Harry Barlow is here already, and so is Sara's Father Lombroso. Stephen and Philippa will be here any minute. See if you can get your sister off the roof. And get some clothes on. Not in that order." To herself she added, "Jesus Christ! This place is like a fucking asylum." What was wrong with these children of hers? Celia wished that they would all come down to earth and simply have dinner: Sara from the damn roof, Adam from his room, Naomi from wherever the hell she was. Ground level: That's where dinner parties happened. Or at least began.

Adam looked toward and through his mother and the garden beyond her, giving her a benign smile, tapping the air, catching its pulse. He would put on his clothes, fetch Sara from the roof. Then he would mingle with the guests, which always sounded pejorative or obscene.

LEAH COHEN SHUFFLED across the grass to the bench at the edge of the woods. Holding the arm of the bench, she lowered herself until she was sitting. Watching Eliza under the birch trees had filled her with undirected yearning. This came so often to her now: wanting without an object, desire without direction or limit of time. When Leah was young her desires had been sharp and focused and temporal. Her pulse would quicken and then came the feeling of hunger mixed with vague melancholy.

Now the whimpers of the shoeless girl in her green socks and burgundy dress brought to mind another sound, thrilling and plaintive, electric almost—the humming of strings, rackets, shuttlecocks. . . .

It had been in Oxford, where she grew up; it was May 1919. Leah had been too tall as a girl, her beaked nose balanced by the masses of dark hair she wore loosely on top of her head. Her friend Miriam, at eighteen, was more cosmopolitan and wore her hair bobbed. The two girls had been painting in the studio, a shed at the back of the garden of Miriam's family's house. It was one of those yearning and gentle days of late spring, suddenly warm, when the air turns greenish yellow, so thick is it with pollen and bloom. Leah had been frustrated by her painting, which had turned puzzling and bothersome, dark, with an immense purple cowslip looming and dangerous in front of the cavern and the distant storm menacing the ships in the sea beyond. She wanted to get away from it. "What about taking a walk?" she said to Miriam, going to the door and looking out. "Or even badminton? There's not a breath of wind." She jabbed her brush into the cup of turpentine and then wiped it on a rag.

Leah and Miriam burst outside, laughing as they ran to the sunporch to get rackets and shuttlecocks. Miriam's family had gone off for the day; the gardener had gone home; it was the cook's day off.

It was natural that in the heat of the May afternoon, as soon as she missed her shot, Leah took off the blue painting smock that covered her clothes. Resuming play, Miriam swung wildly. The birdie went into the net and she in turn used that moment to de-smock.

Perhaps that was what started it. In any case, without either of them saying anything, when Leah next lost a point, she bent down, unstrapped one of her shoes, and placed it by her smock. And Miriam, when she lost, countered with a shoe of her own, tossing it over to the side. Leah forfeited the next shot on purpose to get rid of her other shoe. Miriam soon kicked off her second one to join the others in a heap at the edge of the lawn.

After heated unbuttoning, Leah's blouse of eyelet lace went next, followed by Miriam's high-necked cotton blouse with frills, which had proved anyway to be much too warm.

Green air and giddiness took over, under the hypnotic pluck and whir of flight; for the girls, in giving wing to the feathered cork, had also given it a voice, and when it bounced from their rackets it was as though it were a living thing, whose volition was to go higher and higher into the afternoon sky, and its flight made the strings of the rackets also seem alive, resonating and vibrant.

Soon they were both naked—entirely, stark: full-breasted Leah with her olive-hued skin and long dark hair coming out of its pins, Miriam with her pale skin and bobbed hair, boyish and slim-waisted. Still they kept playing, furiously counting, gasping for points, keeping score.

SOMEWHERE NOW SOME animal barked three times, and this brought Leah back to the Brookline garden where the old wooden bench at the edge of the forest had grown very hard.

This garden had once been hers, these woods and their spring-fed pond. In the rambling three-story house beside the garden she had brought up Pindar and his sisters. In the early years her husband, Gabriel, was there, too. Then he began lecturing in Europe, traveling more and more until it seemed as though he was always saying goodbye. Leah was besieged and tormented with his leaving. Over the years she learned to make a kind of peace with her loneliness, though she never got used to the act of parting. When she turned sixty she gave the house with its woods and gardens to Pindar and his family. Leah was closer to him than to his two sisters, who lived in California. She expected him to telephone almost every day and was delighted each time he did. He still exulted to her about his ideas, his wife, his latest translations of those strange old Mesopotamian recipes, which often didn't seem strange at all.

When she left the house in Brookline, Leah moved to Cambridge; she rather liked living alone. Now that she was in her nineties she had a housekeeper who came in for an hour each weekday, and Pindar had arranged for a girl from Eliot House at Harvard to come on the weekends and help her in the kitchen.

Leah spent her days writing her memoirs and visiting with friends. These elderly ladies, with an occasional listing gentleman in tow, would roam the museums of Cambridge and Boston and then spend lunch together in that delicious fond analytic gossip that records and invents civilization.

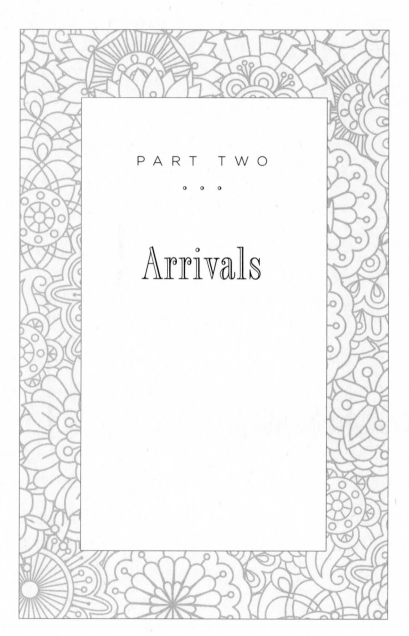

PART TWO

. . .

Arrivals

The stairs in the front hall creak as oaken floorboards talk to nails. Walls shift as the day's warmth rushes out and coolness from the garden flows in to take its place. Couches exhale. In the attic, objects made of suede and velvet stir. Forgotten horsehair mattresses sigh and wonder. Something flutters.

A CAR DOOR slammed. Pindar Cohen stooped and knocked the ashes from his pipe onto a rock, then slid it into his pocket, where the heat of the bowl against his leg spoke of pleasures he could not have until this party was over.

Eliza's parents bore down on him now, marauding tentatively through the garden without noticing the purple haze of lavender, without commenting on the creamy rose with its delirious name. There was no word in English, Pindar realized, for these people, for his relationship to them. He would not call them his mirror in-laws, for that implied a reflection that he did not feel. It wasn't that he didn't like them; he did. But there were so many of them. They brought forth a shyness in him that he didn't know he had. He wanted a word that stressed the distance, their mutual unrelatedness. They were half an hour early. Negative in-laws. Out-laws. They were stealing his time.

Pindar offered his hand, hoping to forestall kisses. Philippa Barlow's bracelets jingled as she took his hand and said something formulaic and kissed him anyway. Stephen Barlow shook hands with hearty and unintelligible mumbles and then patted Pindar's back in a gesture that Pindar found ambiguous. He wondered if it meant that Stephen's being taller implied all sorts of other superiorities—financial, intellectual, moral. Pindar searched for a suitable retort. Instead, he said, "I must say, it's wonderful to see you both." Then he realized that he had seen them that very morning at the wedding rehearsal in the church. "Come," he said. "Let me get you something to drink." With a speed implying medical emergency he escorted them over the grass.

"Gin and tonic . . . here you go. Bourbon for you? There. Listen, this is so rude, but would you two excuse me for just a moment? Can I leave you here in the garden? There's something I have to take care of." Pindar backed away from them, smiling and waving. He refrained from running into the house.

When he had gone, Stephen Barlow said softly, "How cramped these gardens are. No lawns to speak of. No open vistas."

"Not all gardens have open vistas," Philippa whispered. "You know that. You've been here. They don't do lawns, just grassy strips between the nooks and bowers."

"Well, I find these little nooks and bowers limited."

"No, darling. It's you." Philippa paused, then said, "How sudden that was! He looked like a puppet being dragged off-stage." She had no idea that Sara Cohen was overhearing them from the roof. "Strange little man. Like a goat up on hind legs. Apparently he gives brilliant lectures. Isn't that peculiar?"

"Everything is peculiar," said Stephen Barlow.

• • •

INSIDE, PINDAR RAN to the kitchen, where Celia was talking to Chhaya, the cook. The room smelled of chopped scallions, the one member of the alliums not forbidden tonight.

"They're here," Pindar blurted. "Could you . . . ?" He started up the stairs. "I'll be . . ." He gestured toward the garden and hurried up the stairs.

In the bedroom, panting, he lay down on the bed. He just needed to stretch out for half a moment to collect himself. The arrival of guests, particularly ones he wasn't close to, often had this effect on him. *Lots of people run away the moment guests come,* he told himself. *Women go off to the kitchen; I go off to bed. It's very common.*

The shades were closed and the bedroom was dark and sweet. Pindar only meant to rest for a moment, but his lack of sleep the night before made it impossible to stay awake. He dreamed that a man was standing by his head. Although the man's face was turned away from him, Pindar knew he had a long Babylonian beard. The man was telling him something extremely important but before he could make it out someone was tugging at his feet. A gust of wind slammed a door somewhere, and he woke to find a small dark-haired girl pulling at him, saying, "Grandfather. They want you downstairs. The people are here."

When he sat up the girl was gone. As far as he knew, he wasn't anybody's grandfather. Perhaps she was one of Chhaya's nieces. He went to the bathroom and splashed his face with cold water. How long had he been asleep? A quarter of an hour. Celia would be distraught. The buttons of his dark blue shirt had come undone. He combed his gray hair and ran his fingers through his beard. The Barlows had been dressed up. He found a tie, a bright yellow paisley. They would probably notice that he had not been wearing it earlier, but he didn't care. Celia had given it to him, and he needed her hand on him during this dinner. He refused to wear a jacket. It was almost midsummer.

STEPHEN BARLOW'S SON Barnes walked with his wife, Larissa, into the Cohens' garden. Their awkward ten-year-old, Harriet, ran ahead of them, loping with the uneven gait that she had newly adopted, perhaps in order to mirror the discord of her parents. Her wavy black hair was not quite brushed and her white blouse had come untucked. She had always been the sort of child who provokes every passing adult to try to smooth her prickly intelligence and gentle her gaze, but now they wanted to groom and straighten her as well.

Larissa, who had recently taken to calling herself Issa after the Japanese poet, and Barnes, who had always—from childhood and against his will—been called Babar, had been plotting their divorce all morning. Their bitterness toward each other shone on their skin like varnish, coating them inside and out. Barnes was shy and getting shyer. He didn't know if this was the cause of his marital distress or the result. Doubts hovered over him like midges. He no longer made phone calls easily, except to people who would expect no real conversation, just dates and times of meetings, like the dentist or getting his car serviced. He had not told his family that he had just quit his job as a prosecutor in the district attorney's office. How could he argue and declaim in court when all he could really do was mumble. He did not know what would become of him, or of Issa. He feared for his daughter, Harriet: Her mother was venom, her father going mad. He had to get away.

Far ahead of her parents, Harriet galloped up to her grand-mother Philippa Barlow and grabbed her around the hips.

"Oh Lord, child," said Philippa, holding her drink out from her body so as not to spill any on her flowered dress. "Where did you spring from? Where is your hairbrush? What are you doing?"

"Just hugging you. Mummy and Daddy are getting their drinks, but that isn't going to help them. They're in a dreadful mood."

Philippa bent down and smoothed Harriet's black and un-combed hair. "Has no one in your family," she murmured, "ever heard of barrettes or rubber bands?"

"They try, honestly they do. But I keep losing them. It's more than they can handle."

Philippa put her drink down on a flat rock and held on to her granddaughter as though to save them both from drowning. She knew that Barnes and Larissa were in marital upheaval, and presumed it was due to some kind of mischief on Larissa's part. She felt stabbed by their unhappiness and wanted to shield her granddaughter from it.

A sudden breeze carried the sounds from a neighbor's party up the road. Philippa listened, still hugging Harriet and stroking her hair. A jazz trumpet sounded from beyond the woods—joyous and plaintive—along with a sizzle she couldn't identify and the thumping of a drum too low to hear except with her bones.

"AH, CELIA, WAS that your dog we saw as we came in?" asked Philippa Barlow. "What breed is he?"

"Yes, that was Pindar's Adannu. He's part mutt, part mongrel. His name means 'a moment in time' in"—here Celia hesitated and changed course, suspecting that Philippa wouldn't know what Akkadian was—"in one of Pindar's ancient Mesopotamian languages. The cat, who you'll see most often in the garden, is called Shamhat, after a character in the Gilgamesh epic." She decided not to mention that Shamhat was a temple prostitute who civilized the feral Enkidu by means of her sexual artistry. "Do you and Stephen have pets?"

"No cats, but we have a pair of border collies, from the same litter, actually. They're called Talisker and Macallan."

"Oh, I see," said Celia a bit vaguely.

"Single-malt scotches," Philippa said.

"Ah," said Celia with a broad smile.

THE OLDEST BARLOW son, William, and his wife, Olivia, stood off at the side of the lawn. "You got your drink?" said Olivia.

"It's just wine. It seemed too soon for anything else."

"Did you see the garden?"

"Well?"

"Well, for one thing, it's completely gorgeous. In its own odd way."

"It's cluttered, winding; you can barely see the sky," William said.

"Yes, but something is going on. Something—"

William cleared his throat. He always gave a small cough like that to avoid saying what he thought, or simply when embarrassed.

"No, no," Olivia said. "You're wrong. It's not a mess. It's genius."

He gestured here and there with his wineglass.

"Well, you're right, it's taller and more overblown than we're used to." Her voice caught and she hesitated before adding, "It's sort of mysterious, actually. Beautiful. Look at the humor of it."

William looked at his wife. The idea of humor in gardens was not something he was familiar with. He spent his time with war crimes, refugees, international human rights. He said, "Humor."

"Anyway, at least it's not all military array, like your Parisian gardens. None of the lilies are standing at attention."

"Libb, sweetheart, don't start in."

"Right. Well, the surprises, then."

"There has been rain in the past few days," William admitted. "It's green. There are flowers. Do you think they'll have gin?"

"I don't know how to put it. Something strange. One usually doesn't see this sort of thing. Not in a suburban garden."

"Do you think they'll have *decent* gin?"

"The way the path seems to go into a dark passage by the yew but there isn't any way out and suddenly you're face-to-face with the statue."

"What statue?"

"With the head that moves to face you—it seems to, anyway. Some god of the Greeks or Romans. You would know which one it is, you did classics." Olivia led him toward the bluestone path.

They found the statue. "I don't think it moves," William said. "How could it? There isn't any seam. It's carved in stone."

"It must have been the wind making shadows," Olivia conceded.

Olivia had come to hate all things French ever since William had been assigned to the Paris office of his firm and had to go there for several days every month. She knew this was a failing on her part. All wise and reasonable people loved Paris. But she felt suffocated by the formal gardens, maddened by the boulevards, baffled by the language. She was heartsick each time her husband came back from his monthly trips to the Paris office. It was the way he smelled when he returned that made her sad. An intricate and expensive perfume clung to his shirts, his skin, his fair hair. That scent turned him into a stranger who tried to mimic the gestures and voice of Will Barlow. If she knew the name of this fragrance, that wouldn't make anything more bearable, she knew that. Still, she had searched, haunting and sniffing at department store perfume counters until the smell of any perfume at all made her retch. Unable to find the name, she had denied herself permission to mention it to him.

"The French," she said whisking her fingers through the pinkish lace of a bloom with no fragrance. "I know. I'm sorry. But this place is so astonishing. Look at that tall feathery thing. No. Above you . . ." How could he not see it? "Which of them created it, do you think, Pindar or Celia?"

"We could ask them," William said.

Olivia could see that he was relieved at the way they had skirted the topic of Parisian gardens, part of the geography of the unspoken and unspeakable.

He touched her arm to make peace. "It would be something to talk about." The only thing they had been able to agree on while driving in from Concord was their not knowing what they would talk about with the Cohens.

Olivia took his hand.

An almost invisible bird, a small piece of hopping dirt, purposed along the edge of the flower bed, eyeing for beauty or looking for worms. Olivia watched it as she walked with her husband toward the yew and the puzzling statue. *We count those birds as nothing,* she thought, *the small dun-colored ones, and prefer to keep our wonder for the spectral glory of cardinals, or the ungainly grace of cranes. Goldfinches and even jays delight us, but are they so different from these common little brown birds which we think of as vermin? Astonishing accidents of pigment, size, plumage: Why do they elicit our wonder?*

"HOLD ON, ELIZA. Settle down. I know what to do."

Eliza, usually solid and clear-eyed and calm, was blotchy with bridal panic. Thoughts of tomorrow's pomp and spectacle had spooked her. She was sitting on a stone bench at the end of the garden, between her twin brother, Harry, and her beloved, Adam.

"Look, sweetheart," Adam said, kissing her on the ear. He nodded at Harry. "We have our minister here. Why don't we elope?"

"What do you mean?"

"Right here, now, up in the attic."

Eliza looked up. "Elope in the attic of your house? How? What about the wedding tomorrow?"

"We do it now, in the attic, and that will just be for us. At the other wedding, tomorrow, we will go through the forms, to give pleasure to the parentals. The one right now is what counts."

"So they will think they are watching us get married?" She

looked at Adam. She gave a tentative smile. "Hal? An attic wedding? Can you?"

"That is what attics are for," said Harry.

They asked Leah, Adam's ancient grandmother, to be their witness. She was dressed this evening in dark mauve and held herself with the straightness of a marble column. For her, posture was not a task, as it was for the inebriate, the unwell, the pained. She had never had trouble with her back. She did not take naps. They had heard that she had been sent from England to Paris in the dangerous and grief-astounded 1920s—to paint. It was said that she tore men apart, and women. Now, in her nineties, Leah appeared to them courteous and formal and harrowing, knotted by scars of loss and strengthened by love. It was Leah, they knew, who had named Adam's father Pindar and had taught him Hebrew and Greek when he was a child. Pindar's father, also a classical scholar, had always been mostly absent, appearing at rare moments, unannounced and sometimes inconvenient.

"Terrific!" said Leah. "Eloping is the only way to go. Of course I can make it up the attic stairs. Better cart me off right now if I can't. I would be honored to be your witness. As for secrecy, you will find me silent as the hour before dawn. But what about your sisters, Adam? Shouldn't we get Sara off the roof?"

When they got up to the attic, Adam went to the window and opened it, whistling softly at Sara. He sat on the ledge and leaned out so that he could see her better.

"Hey," she said, swiveling around to look down at him.

"Hey, yourself," he answered. "What are you doing up there?"

"Watching all of you," she said. "Did they send you up here

to get me to come down and mingle? I know it's horribly rude of me to stay here, but the light is too perfect." She gave a smile that forgave everything, demanded forgiveness, and knew that one could hope for but not demand such a thing.

"Of course they told me to come and get you to mingle, but I've got something much better in mind, a much better invitation."

"To join you all down there."

"Yes, that is a possibility."

"I'm not much of a joiner," she said, waving a hand as though to flick the idea away.

"I know," he said.

Sara had always been solitary in her interests and passions. All through their adolescence he would chastise her for it. *You silly,* he would say. *Don't be such a lonely ecstatic.* And yet he had always found this aloneness of Sara's attractive. His younger sister Naomi was the opposite, collecting strays when she couldn't find a humanitarian group to join.

"You know," he said, sweetly teasing. "We could *all* come up there and join you. We could bring our supper and our wine." He looked down at the ground and felt slightly giddy.

Sara laughed. "You would turn to jelly up here on the roof. Aside from that, it's a lovely idea. But what's your *better* invitation?"

"Lizzie and I are eloping. Right now. Here in the attic. Come in and join us?"

"My friend Dennis is here. Should I get him?"

"Actually, we're all up here and we've got to be really quick. Is that okay?"

"Of course," she said. "Besides, you two haven't even met yet." She unfolded herself and stood slowly and shook her legs to wake them up. Then she stepped along the slates to the dormer window where Adam was sitting. As he got up from the windowsill she climbed inside to join him.

IN THE ATTIC, Adam pulled the string of the single lightbulb dangling from the rafters. The room smelled of sun on old wood and unexpected spices. Turning to his grandmother, he said, "Is it too hot for you? Let me open more windows."

"Air would be lovely," said Leah. "But we have to be quick and not too rowdy, so they don't hear us."

Adam opened the dormer windows on the other side of the tall peaked room.

"You see, Liz?" Harry said. "We can do it right here."

Again Eliza smiled. Perhaps they had found the way out. They stood under the embroidered bedspread that Adam's parents had brought back from India several years earlier and had hung over two beams to air out. The red and gold cloth hovered over them, glinting with little mirrors, shifting now in the breeze from the windows. It smelled of fenugreek and clove, as though the aromatic powders from the bazaar had been trapped behind the tiny mirrors to be released only when the cloth was touched or shaken by the wind. Leah held one of its corners, rubbed it between bony fingers. "Your grandfather Gabriel, Pindar's father, loved this smell . . . ," she began. Then, remembering what they were gathered for, "Sorry, dears. Another time."

"It should only take a few minutes," Harry said. "I'll cut whatever I can. You've got the rings?"

"Damn. Can we do it without? They're down in my room."

"It's best to get them," Harry said. "You see, there's always this question of where the actual ceremony resides—for Christians it happens during the vows, but for the Jews it's during the exchange of rings. For Jews, if one of you dies right after you give each other the rings but before other things are said, it's okay. You're married."

Adam ran downstairs. He came back, slightly winded, with the two small leather boxes and gave them to Sara.

"You are all," Harry began, "my dearly beloved."

Eliza bit her lip. Adam fingered the pencil in his pocket then put his hand on Eliza's shoulder.

"We are gathered here in the sight of God, and of this witness." Harry raised his eyes, then added, "and of this small dark bat . . ."

Eliza shook her head.

". . . to join together this man and this woman in marriage, a sacred and joyous covenant, ordained by God, signifying a mystical union—not to be entered into lightly, but reverently, discreetly, soberly, and in the fear of God."

Eliza put up her hand.

Harry stopped. "What is it, Liz? You said that 'God' would be okay."

"No, no. It's not that. It's the bat: It's called a big brown bat. Also, I'm piss drunk. Will it still count?"

"Your mind when you decided to marry was sober. Your flesh just happens not to be, at the moment. Most people are out of their heads during the actual ceremony. I can leave out 'soberly' if you like."

"Hurry, my dears," Leah said. "These things have to be quick."

But there was no time for Harry to reword anything. The attic door opened and his mother stood at the threshold, observing the scene. Philippa Barlow refrained from stepping in, as though the room were sacred or unclean. "There you are," she said. "Everybody's been looking all over for you, Eliza, Harry, Adam. Hello, Sara. Surely you can practice your charades later. Oh, Leah, I didn't see you. Imagine dragging poor old Mrs. Cohen all the way up here."

"Oh, they didn't drag me, dear. I climbed most willingly and on my own two feet."

Philippa looked as though she didn't know what to reply. She turned and went down the stairs. Chagrined and docile, the clandestine wedding party followed her from the attic. Adam turned out the light. As soon as his mother was out of hearing, Harry said, "Meet at the pond in ten minutes. We can finish up there."

HEAT DRIFTS UP from men and women standing by the drinks table. The bracelets on the perfumed woman's arm and the gold chains around her neck bounce spangles of light and sound.

WHEN PINDAR CAME back outside after his nap, he found his garden taken over by three generations of Barlows. Celia had given them all drinks. She was helped in this by Borsuk, who had transformed himself for the evening into an old-world butler. This had shocked the Cohens, but they did not know what to do or say. Weeks earlier, when Pindar had asked him to help out with the dinner party, he had wondered if Borsuk would put on clean clothes but had not dared to suggest it. Now the gardener had found himself a tuxedo, and he hovered about looking knowing and clean and helpful, with well-scrubbed fingernails and a bit of pomade in his collar-length graying hair.

Pindar found Celia and leaned toward her. He wanted to give her a kiss, but he didn't want this to be observed by the Barlows. "I fell asleep," he muttered. "How long was I gone?"

"Eons," she whispered, bending toward him. "The first minutes are always sticky."

"That's why I had to leave."

"It seemed like they all got here at once. I think it was choreographed—so none of them had to be with us alone."

"Sara? Is she down yet?"

"Finally. I saw her with Adam and Eliza."

"Naomi?"

"No sign."

STEPHEN BARLOW WATCHED the group of young people following Philippa out of the Cohen house. How furtive they were. Adam with his bewildered eyes, deep-set, circled and liverish. The young woman beside him was probably his sister, Sara, who did something with some sort of pests. She had the same red hair as her brother, only brighter. There was a younger sister, somewhat strange—he had met her once, briefly, but she had not appeared yet. His own lovely Elizabeth looked a bit of a mess. As though she'd been crying, though she was not that sort. He had never really understood his daughter's choice to work with animals. Large animals, small brains. Or was it small animals, small brains? And his son Harry. He sometimes wondered whether, perhaps because they were twins, Harry and Eliza had each only received half the normal brain allotment. Of course he loved them, but it was harder to be proud of these two. His three older boys were robust and straightforward and adult. He had never been able to pin Harry down and get him to say exactly what he was doing and exactly what he believed. Leaving law school for seminary, and then to be sent down for something undisclosed. A private matter, the dean had said. And then the boy had sidestepped into another seminary on the West Coast. Possibly it wasn't even Christian. Harry darted among disciplines as shamelessly as that bat up there flinging itself on the purple flowers that hung down from the eaves.

Stephen Barlow was very conscious of his position as father of the bride. He kept trying to warm to these Cohens, but it would have been much easier if only they realized how strange they were. Celia, the dumpy little woman with Brillo for hair: Could she really be a good critic of English literature when she spoke with an Eastern European accent and dressed like a farmer's wife? And the husband, *Pindar,* for Christ's sake, standing there hunched, chewing on his own lips. He studied obscure or nonexistent languages, unknown to Athens or Rome and lacking any halfway decent literature. What was the point of building even a brilliant life around fragments? What did that have to do with practical contributions to society? What good did Celia's literary criticism do, in the scheme of things? It wasn't just that the whole family was so academic, nor that they were all so physically strange: Pindar, with his patriarchal beard and the posture of a buzzard, Celia with her billows of hair and bosom, Adam with those haunted shadows under his eyes, Sara with her exotic interests, angular Naomi—was that her name?—with her look of private startle. It was that their view was limited. This was what made academics so peculiar, of course, and here was a whole family of them. It stood to reason that one was condemned to putter or dabble if one spent one's whole time nosing around texts that had no real use and could not see further than the page. It was sad, Stephen Barlow felt, the way these Cohens were missing out on the vastness and clarity of the real. He and Pippa and their three older sons were bathed in this clarity. The documents they spent their time with all led immediately to societal covenants and the way people interacted with one another. He with his corporations, Pippa with her estates, William, their eldest and the one he was proudest of, in international law, then Cameron in intellectual property and young Barnes forging ahead in prosecution: They all knew how humans connected, across the continents and down the ladders of the generations. They knew what people did to and for one another. Every day they talked with people who bared their holdings if not their hearts, which they often hid with great deviousness and guile. But these were actual people, or corporations acting as people, not glimpses of clay shards with their ambiguous scratches and poke-marks, not serpents or insects or whatever they were, not squawks and rhymes and prayers. Pippa, for example, could calculate in a glance the tax burden on the Cohen property here, could estimate the whole estate before and after the death of the elder Cohens. Nothing of terrific value within the house, though Pindar's mother, Mrs. Leah Cohen, was rumored to be linked somehow to the English branch of one of the great Jewish banking families. Stephen Barlow had discounted this gossip until he caught sight of the small photograph in the Cohens' front hall of a four-in-hand carriage drawn by two teams of zebras, although when he looked more closely he could make out that the left front animal was not a zebra but a black horse. Eliza would know if that was where you put the lead animal, and if you needed a horse for that spot, a horse perhaps being more tractable than a zebra? Rather eccentric, wasn't it, to drive zebras? Was it *original*? Or was it simply a hobby for the overmoneyed and underemployed? But then all hobbies, like all obsessions, made little sense to outsiders. He would get to know these people, but he wished there was some way to do it without all these festivities, some way one could get them to really sit down and have a decent chat about things that mattered.

Stephen Barlow inhaled happily as his three older sons strode into the garden talking of the hurried nine holes they had just played. He would invite them out for a foursome tomorrow. He wanted to play all day with them. They humored him, but he let them, for it was one of the main ways that he knew his sons; not that they talked much out on the course—they didn't try to bring conversation in—it was more that they revealed themselves by stance and swing and gesture in a way that seemed unself-conscious and almost animal in its naturalness. Hell's bells. Tomorrow was the damned wedding. No golf unless the boys would consent to get up at six. And Pippa was in such a state.

Stephen Barlow was pouring another gin and tonic for Pippa at the wobbly wooden table in the Cohens' garden. "It's like a third-world country here," he said softly.

"Whatever do you mean?"

"No *Wall Street Journal* on the front hall table. No *Economist*."

"Good Lord. You're not here to inspect their reading matter."

"No front hall table, even," Stephen went on. "There's just a grotesque tree stump, gnarled and indented. It's smoothed and polished, so it was probably placed there, not blown in by the last hurricane, but you can't be sure. There is a pile of mail on it. But it is not a table," he said.

"Oh?"

"I promise you it is not a table."

"Oh, darling. Do dry up," Philippa replied. "How can you be so narrow-minded? A proper table in the front hall is not really a marker of the developed world." Then, conciliatory, she asked him, "Whatever are we going to talk to them about?"

"I know what you mean," he said. "It's a bit like being among the forest animals. Do you think the dinner will be acorns and grubs?"

"Oh, stop."

"Yes, that's what I mean: Do you think there's any way of stopping it? Do you think Lizzie's going to be happy with them?"

PHILIPPA BARLOW WAS frightened by all the members of the Cohen family, even Pindar's mother, Leah, who did not seem to have been properly neutralized by her extreme age. Pippa had heard that Leah was over a hundred. Could that be? Could such people come to wedding rehearsal dinners? Could they still chew their food? Even Leah had done something anomalous, Pippa couldn't remember what it was exactly—before the war? between the wars?—in Paris or London. Eliza had told her that none of the Cohens rode, or played any sort of games. What was life like without games? Probably they played word games requiring obscure dictionaries. But those weren't actual games, that was just talking while sitting. She wondered if dictionaries would appear at the table tonight, as party favors or instead of dessert.

Pippa's sister, Charlotte, had told her over lunch about a new article that Celia Cohen had just published somewhere. "The woman is startlingly brilliant," Charlotte had said. "God, Pips, I don't know how you even dare speak to her." Pippa would have preferred not to know this about her hostess. The article had been about an aging New York poet nobody could understand, something about yellow tulips, and that other one, a Scot with his pitchforks, or was he a Welshman? If only Charlotte would get here, then Pippa could relax and travel in her wake. But Charlotte always came late to parties; she liked them to be well oiled and smoothly rolling before she showed up.

It was perplexing to Philippa that her only daughter, her Eliza, should be so wildly other. What on earth would she do with a poet? Adam Cohen with his owl eyes was sweet and clearly loved Eliza. He had even demanded that she make a prenuptial agreement with him, which no one had expected, but he was unsettled in life and thus unsettling. True, he had just landed a job at Wellesley, but poets did not really support families; they drank themselves to death and then jumped off bridges. Philippa knew that Eliza was unusual: Animals worshipped her. She attracted them even though she dressed like a heretic. Even that dog of the Cohens had followed her out of the woods. The girl must give off some smell or vibration that attracted the beasts to her. But that she should then turn around and follow *them,* taking care of distemper or peering into hooves and mouths and reaching into unthinkable places for difficult births? If Eliza really insisted on making her life among steamy dung heaps, hardscrabbling in squalor with poets, well, there was nothing for Philippa to do but to send her off to her new life in beauty. In white. When that was done, then possibly the bear trap of worry that for years now had clamped between Philippa's shoulders would let go. She pulled her shoulders up to her ears, then rotated them back and down, trying to loosen her machinery.

"ARE YOU STIFF? Shall I rub?" Cameron, Philippa's favorite, had come up behind her. He massaged her shoulders. He did this partly to soothe his mother, and partly because he felt guilty for having done a bit of exploring in the Cohens' house. He had been looking for the bathroom and, missing the one by the stairs, found himself upstairs in Celia's study. He felt perverse but almost justified in this trespass, welcoming the chance to figure out who these people were, this clan that his sister, Eliza, was marrying into. Five minutes alone in someone's room, poking through their books and their papers, could tell you more than any number of cheese cubes and cocktails.

The smell, for one thing. Celia's study smelled of some pungent flower—he didn't know the name, slightly astringent—and the roasted-paper smell of very old books, and the seared ink of photocopied pages. There were stacks of papers, neat cardboard files, filing cabinets. He hadn't expected so much order, or that her computer would be the most recent model. A gray writing book with green spine and corners sat beside it. He turned to the last entry; it was dated three days earlier:

Of course when we open a novel there's the sudden
hovering presence of the author—a spirit inhabiting our
room, talking into our mind's ear. This ghostly presence
is what is meant by ES when she talks of authorial
instruction. She talks of vivacity of the scene we imagine

under such instruction. But even the authors, even the dead authors—don't they, too, have a certain vivacity? What is the nature of this whispering companion?

WEDDING PARTY:

- Tell Borsuk to mow garden first, then the back meadow; clip roses by gate; check fishpond for dead.
- Take dog for shampoo.
- Cut Pindar's hair.
- Check wine. Will they need gin?
- Naomi???

Cameron smiled at the note about gin. He was part of "they," but he preferred wine, although his parents would need the gin, and his brothers, except for Hal. He didn't know what Hal drank. Absinthe.

Turning the page, Cameron found the seating plan for that night's dinner. An earlier arrangement had been crossed out: It showed two tables, all the Barlows at one, the Cohens at the other. In the latest version, Cameron noted that Adam's sister Naomi was to be opposite him. She was the youngest. There was some mystery about her, some shame or glory.

After finding the bathroom, Cameron went downstairs and drifted into a book-lined room. There were three leather reading chairs, each with its own standing lamp. Three hassocks. A long greenish couch, a bit clawed on the edges. Pindar's study opened off from this room. Here was the chaos Cam had been expecting. Lingering pipe smoke. A boxy computer fought for space among splayed books and papers on the desk. An ashtray filled with spent tobacco floated like a raft on the top layer of mess.

Cameron looked up suddenly, feeling that he was being watched. But it was only a statue, in the corner: a shockingly graceful tree trunk carved into a limbless torso, with a marble head, a perfect oval, on top. Heroic in size, Greek in stillness. Contemplative. But it filled Cam with questions: How was the head attached? Would the whole thing topple if pushed? What was it doing there? A warm breeze lifted the curtains behind the desk.

"What are you doing here?"

Cameron jumped back. "Hello. Who are you?" Always best to question the questioner, in this case a girl who looked to be about nine years old. She had the smooth dark hair and translucent face of a child who spends too much time indoors.

"Are you from here?"

"That depends, doesn't it?"

"Well, are you on our side or their side?"

"Which is which?" he asked.

"Are you looking for books in broken languages?"

"Not really," he said. "Are you? Do you read them?"

"No. But they are here. I'm ten. I had an illness. Sometimes I still feel like a bletted medlar. If you know what I mean."

"Not exactly," said Cameron.

"Medlar, with an *a*," the girl said.

"I still don't."

"It's a fruit," she explained. "Ripe and wretched."

"I see." He paused. "Shouldn't we be joining the others?"

"Run along, then," she said, as though he were the child. "I shouldn't really be here; I started out in a different gathering, but it was too loud and I like this one better. Perhaps I'll join you in the fullness of time."

Cameron retreated to the dining room, then down the steps

to the garden, where he found his mother looking stiff in the shoulders.

Outside, standing by the makeshift drinks table, Philippa Barlow raised a gold-braceleted arm to her head. Something veered and flapped. "Why are the bats out so early? Is that the one we saw before?" she asked.

"I don't think so," said Barnes, her third-born, who sighed all the time these days. "That one's still up there in the trellis; see it all folded and crimped?"

"Where's Eliza gone to?"

"I don't know. Harry's off somewhere, too. And Adam."

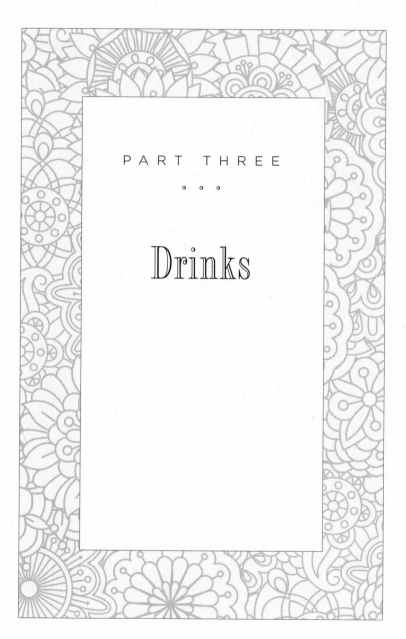

PART THREE

. . .

Drinks

S

een from above, the canopy of oak and maple and pine is pierced by the pond, which looks back at you like some green eye, knowing and ancient. The air above the pond dives into clefts of coolness, then rises up at the warmth of the margins. Down the path, filigrees of blackflies and mosquitoes dance in the heat waves given off by men and women and their domestic fires. Joyous bats dart about.

STRAIGHT AS A goddess, Leah sat on the old stone bench beside the pond, witnessing the new attempt at the clandestine wedding. Her granddaughter Sara sat beside her. Young Harry Barlow stood facing Adam and Eliza, who had a look of tentative mischief. In the undergrowth robins sang of water; in the rushes bullfrogs croaked of love. The cardinal whistled to his mate. As Harry rushed through the ritual words, Leah wondered what he would look like clothed only in leaves. His hair was so dark it was almost blue. Could he dance? she wondered. She would follow if he started any dance at all. She could see him wreathed with grapes, standing on a boat with curving prow, the mast encircled with vines, all the sailors already transformed into dolphins. Leah gazed at Harry and plucked absentmindedly at the ivy growing over the bench.

"... lawfully be married, speak ..."

"Stop! Come back! Eli!" came the strident call of a ten-year-old girl. "You can't go there! Grandma said we mustn't go to the pond. Besides, it's got poisonous frogs. If they touch you, you'll die . . . certainly before morning."

The intruder was Laurie, William and Olivia Barlow's daughter, chasing her little brother, Eliot, who had run silently up to the water's edge.

"Hello, Uncle Harry, what are you doing?" chattered Laurie. "Auntie Eliza, Grandma Pipps said that if we find you we should tell you to come back to the party in the garden or she'll . . . chop your toes off with a guillotine."

Eliza's bare toes clenched. Adam put his arm around her. Resigned to this latest interruption, Harry folded his notes for the ceremony and put them in his pocket. He smiled and offered his arm to Leah, who lifted herself from the bench and stood like a caryatid. She held on to Harry as the young children shepherded the adults back to the party.

Laurie said to Eliza, "Grandma doesn't understand why you can't simply mingle. She says it's God's own duty. At parties."

Returning from the pond, Harry tried to walk sedately holding Leah Cohen's arm. Her purple silk dress fell in swooping layers. He couldn't tell if it was very old-fashioned or extremely modern. Adam and Eliza followed them, still holding hands. Laurie was in the lead, while little Eli raced around the four adults. He was three years old and had never, in public, talked. He appeared to be clever, he could grunt and laugh and babble, but he would not say a word. William and Olivia Barlow took him to speech clinics where the experts said not to worry, that often these things straightened themselves out in time—as though the little boy's larynx was knotted or kinked and simple elongation due to growth would fix it. His parents had learned to avoid mentioning Eliot's muteness. William, who blamed himself for the boy's silence, tried not to think about this problem. Olivia worried about it constantly.

PHILIPPA BARLOW WAS delighted when her father, Nathan Morrill, asked her to take him to the kitchen so that he could watch the cooking. His presence at the party, while necessary, was also a bother. He fumbled and spilled—no fault of his own, poor devil—and had a tendency to leer at the girls and women. Philippa was relieved to be able to put him aside for a bit.

"This is Mr. Morrill," Philippa said to the small Asian woman with the odd-looking meat cleaver. "Would he be in your way here if he watched you cook for a bit?"

"He's fine here," said Chhaya, who took one look at him and thought, *Poor old monkey*. She put down her knife and told the old man her name. "Where I come from it means 'shadow,'" she added. "And also 'light.'"

Philippa settled her father in a chair.

Nathan Morrill was only eighty-nine, but in him a process of unweaving had begun. His appreciation at times outran his comprehension. He still delighted in his everyday pleasures but didn't always understand the links and connections that brought them about. Some days, he forgot where coffee came from—the kitchen, surely, but before that? Some days he ate his butter separately from his toast. But then sometimes he faked this opacity, so as not to have to deal with things. And sometimes he simply hurt all over and brilliance or even translucence was not something he could imagine or invoke. Today, however, was one of his good days, and he held on to clarity with a fierce greed.

As soon as Philippa had gone, Borsuk appeared. "Here," said Chhaya, holding out a stalk of asparagus to him. "Tell me what you think."

"One moment," said Borsuk. Going to the sink, he washed his hands. Then, taking the stalk, he ate it and smiled. "Perfect," he said.

"Would you like a drink?" Chhaya said to Nathan Morrill.

"Oh. Bless you. What do you have?"

"What would you like?"

He squinted at her. "What are they hiding?"

"You mean from the guests?" she said. "They don't hide liquor, here. Just chocolates: the El Rey and the Bendicks. Impossible to buy now, only from England."

"I'll have some scotch whiskey, then, and some El Rey."

"Sorry about the chocolates. Cannot do. Scotch, yes."

Nat Morrill stood up.

His lurching manner startled Chhaya. She backed around the kitchen island, keeping it between her and the old man, who grinned as he shambled toward her, fumbling at his pocket with a hand that seemed too large to find its way in. Extricating his wallet, Morrill poked with stiff straight fingers in the bill compartment. "Here you are, my dear," he said, taking out a twenty-dollar bill. "Would you kindly give us chocolate?"

Chhaya appeared not to see what he had done and went to the cupboard to get a glass for his whiskey. "Ice, sir?"

"Too old for ice: pierces new channels in all the ancient fangs. But I do need the El Rey." He flicked the bill against his fingers. Chhaya did not look. He tapped the money in his palm.

"No bribes," she said. "Not from strangers." She handed him the drink. "Most people do not know about El Rey."

He looked at her sharply to see if the word *strangers* was an invitation of some sort. Should he offer to know her better? "Where are you from, my dear? Where is your family?"

"Basically, not matters for discussion," she said, standing still and straight.

He lifted his glass with both hands and drank. "Forgive me," he said. "I am an offensive old turkey. If you would let me sit here and watch while you cook, it would give me indescribable pleasure. I will play quietly with my drink. If I cannot be from time to time in a working kitchen, my soul gets derailed. I was a great cook in my day." He paused and held his drink up to the light, then gulped at it. "Do they have gingerbread where you come from? I'll wager you had green ginger with your mother's milk, but in savory form, not sweet. Not gingerbread. Not in your country."

"This is my country now," Chhaya said quietly. "I know your gingerbread."

"I doubt you know my exact gingerbread," he replied. "You see, mine has three gingers: powdered—which is an abomination, but it's in there; fresh—at least half a cup, minced fine or grated; and finally crystallized—for nuggets of burning clarity."

"What else?" Chhaya said, alert now, as though setting it all down on the chalkboard of her mind.

"Molasses, an egg, a stick of butter, flour. Sugar. The usual. Your everyday risers."

"What sugar?"

"Brown," he said. "From Mauritius, if you can find it. It has a bit of depth to it, a wildness."

"And?"

"That's it. That's all there is."

"What makes it . . . splendid? What secret do you leave out when you tell me?"

"Ah. Splendors. Take a guess."

"Galangal?"

"Nope. It should be tried, but I haven't."

"Lemongrass?"

"That would be genius; but it wasn't that."

"White pepper?"

"Yes," he said, putting his empty glass on the table and smiling. "My gingerbread had white pepper and three gingers and my God but it would always triumph. Now I lurk about in other people's kitchens and do not cook. Mostly my arms and legs ache like branches in an ice storm. Invisible creatures hide in my joints and shoot venom into my hinges when I move. A few years ago I was bitten by a tick as small as a poppy seed, and its poison has made the slow voyage to my brain." He paused, rubbing a large hand over his thin white hair, then added, "I was probably just as offensive before, but possibly in a different way."

Chhaya went to the cupboard and broke off a corner of the block of El Rey. She brought it over to him and put it in his hand. He seemed not to notice but slowly he brought it to his mouth, jabbed it toward his teeth, nibbled at it. A smile like a slow enlightenment came over his face. "Did you ever wonder," he said, "why some places have signs in their windows saying 'Breakfast all day,' while no place informs you 'We serve dinner at dawn'?"

THE WIND RUSTLES through the birches bringing a few notes of a once-joyful trumpet. The linen tablecloth ripples for a moment as though trying to escape. Then the breeze dies down. The music is gone. The white cloth is still.

• • •

THE YOUNG GIRL whose skin was almost too fair tugged on Philippa's dress, but Philippa was talking to her son William, and either didn't feel it or chose not to turn around. So the girl drifted over to Celia. "Excuse me, but do you think I could have a cup of tea?"

"Why of course, child," said Celia. "Who do you belong to?"

The girl made a vague gesture toward the edge of the garden and the forest beyond, where the music had come from.

"I see. . . . Well, go into the kitchen and ask Chhaya."

Pindar's dog followed the girl to the kitchen, where Nathan Morrill was dozing in the corner. Adannu sat by the old man and slapped his tail on the floor, keeping time. The rhythmic noise woke Morrill, who watched and kept silent.

"May I please have a cup of tea?"

Hearing the child's voice, Chhaya did not look up but said, "Actually, there is a punch for children. It is outside. Would you like?"

"Heavens, no."

Chhaya turned around. "Oh," she said, putting down her chopping knife. "Oh. I'll boil the water. What would you like, black or green?"

"Green, please. It has an earthier taste."

"What is your name?"

"Leila. It means 'evening,' but I would rather have a morning name. I was at the other party, but I like your party better."

"I see. Cup or mug?"

"Cup, please. The best china. Gold-rimmed, no flowers. No cracks or chips. It's okay. I don't break things."

When the tea was ready, Chhaya poured it out for the girl and gave it to her. Leila walked slowly out of the kitchen toward the library.

"Well, I'll be damned," said Nat Morrill.

Chhaya put her palms together and brought them to her forehead.

CELIA COHEN WALKED to the driveway when she heard a car door slam. She gave one last look at the green of the garden and tried to see it all not as work that needed to be done but as the glory that it already was. She wondered if her feelings about the Barlows were too sure. She did not want to lose what she thought of as salubrious doubt about them. She knew that she was too sure she understood them and found them lacking, in depth, in delight, in their ability to surprise her or themselves. Yet doubt itself was the basis on which she judged others, though it was so fundamental that she wasn't always conscious of it. "Has this person gotten there?" she would ask herself, meaning "Has he achieved doubt?" But now she herself had jettisoned all unsureness where the Barlows were concerned. In the face of their seeming lack of doubt she had forgotten to hold on to her own.

Philippa Barlow's younger sister introduced herself. "I am Charlotte Morrill, Eliza's aunt."

"Of course, I remember you," said Celia, ratcheting up her cordiality. Charlotte wrote for the newspaper and dressed for downtown. Celia threw herself into her greeting as though Charlotte were a messenger not from *The Boston Globe* but farther off. "We met in September, at the university library, actually. It was the reception for our poet in residence. I didn't realize then that you were Eliza's aunt."

"Yes," Charlotte said, startled. "You were wearing gray with a silver necklace. And we talked a bit about telescopes and the infinite. I don't know why we talked about that, but I think it was something you had been reading." She paused and gave a little laugh. "Unless it was something I had been reading. I never remember what I read." Charlotte looked at Celia and thought that probably *she* remembered everything she had ever read or heard or thought. She appraised Celia's hair, which had the texture of steel wool, and her necklace, which was lovely and uncommon—Eastern Europe, between the wars, with a complex ornament in the middle, set with emeralds. It would be nice to get a photo of it. Perhaps at the end of tonight's dinner, after too much wine. Clearly Celia wore this necklace often—Charlotte could tell when something was being paraded for an event—but how strange to wear such a beguiling jewel when one's own shape was that of a feather bed. Eiderdown. Oh, the lugging of the mindless flesh. Poor woman probably prayed to be reborn as a serpent.

HALOES OF HEAT shimmer from the guests and their hosts. The candles burn brighter. The plump flies of dusk now congregate around the plates of cheese and crackers on the wooden table. From the cut glass bowl of children's punch, sweet rosy fumes spiral up into the air.

EIGHT-YEAR-OLD EMILY, daughter of Cameron and Amy Barlow—already the fierce lover of insects she would always be—used her finger to paint a trail of punch from the glass bowl, across the table and down one of the legs, in hopes of luring ants. Nearby, Eliza stood on one leg, leaning against a tree, as she instructed Charlotte Morrill.

"Not the wedding tomorrow, Auntie Char. Okay?"

"Of course."

"And not tonight's dinner."

"Not tonight, I promise. I am here as family. Any photos I take are not for the paper. They're for you and Adam, period."

Charlotte was only occasionally defensive about writing about "society" for *The Boston Globe*. She claimed that she went after "the borderline philanthropic," goading them by her presence: She said she had the power to nudge and finally topple them into acts of great generosity—knowing that they would find, the next day, in her news columns, their own dowdy selves transformed by her photographs and their ordinary attributes tinseled by her sparkling and perhaps overheated prose.

A cloud of mosquitoes and blackflies hovered above Eliza's hair but did not bite her. She was like the patch of zinc on the hull of a motor yacht, attracting the charged particles of seawater onto itself and keeping them away from the brass propeller, where they would otherwise attach, react, and corrode.

Now her brother Cameron's children clustered around Eliza as well. Both had strawberry-blond hair. Emily with her open gaze, and seven-year-old Liam, already sultry, draped themselves against Eliza's arms, mantling her with their bodies. Eliza's aunt Charlotte watched them, musing at the unearned beauty of the young.

"IT'S GETTING LATE," said Celia to Adam. "Could you go find Naomi? See if she'll make it to dinner."

Naomi had been home from Bucharest now for six weeks, and at times she seemed totally fine, Celia thought, though fragile. Her two daughters were so different. Both girls had gone to the Amazon while in college, though not with each other. While Naomi, the younger, traveled on the malaria boats throbbing their way to distant hamlets along the river, Sara was trekking in the rain forest with her then boyfriend, an ethnobotanist, gathering scorpions and sampling hallucinogens by means of blowpipes up the nostrils. Sara knew so much, knew many of the wrong things, much that was forbidden. Unusual knowledge clung to her, as though strangeness were sewn into the hem of her skirts.

Both girls were so complicated, Celia thought, though Naomi's mission seemed much simpler. With Naomi things were so clear. She was concerned with action, not knowledge: In South America she administered antimalarials; in Romania she took care of orphans; at home she tended to the dying. But now, for the past few days, she had taken to her room, coming out only for meals. It was not clear to Celia if Naomi would join tonight's prenuptial dinner, but if anyone could convince her to come out of her room it was her brother. "Go, dear," Celia told Adam again. "Persuade her."

"NOME, IT'S ME," Adam said. "Can I come in?"

"Of course. It's not locked." Naomi stood in the middle of the room, dressed in a camisole and panties. Her hair, which for some reason she had clipped off in Bucharest, had grown back in the six weeks she'd been home. She looked elfin now, rather than shorn, but she had not yet gained back all her weight and she seemed a bit too slender. "Oh God," she said. "Sorry for the mess." The floor around her was strewn with skirts and dresses; underwear littered the bed.

"Oh, it's not so bad," he lied. The mess was disturbing. Naomi was usually painfully neat. "So. What's up? Laundry?"

"I can't find a thing to wear."

"But, Nome . . ."

"I'm trying to get them to fit. They've all gotten so loose." She picked up a yellow sundress and slipped it over her head, then looked at herself in the mirror. She tiptoed back and forth, then curtsied in front of him, holding the skirt of her dress. "Sweet, simple, and girlish," she said. "But I used to like the way the straps cross in back. Look," she said. Gripping the waistband, she showed Adam how loose it was on her. "While I was gone in Romania, my clothes grew. They've turned into bags. I think they want to be someone else's clothes, not mine. This 'yellow milkmaid' number is impossible." She stripped down to camisole and panties again.

"Nome?"

Naomi inhaled, then let her breath out in a rush. "I know, I know. This is nuts."

"I just want . . ."

"You want me to come to the wedding."

"Of course I do. But first there's the rehearsal dinner. To-night. Sort of—now. All the Barlows—"

"Oh God. Here? Even Vicious Grandpa?"

"He's not vicious. He's my favorite. At times he's still incredibly interesting, though at other times he seems a bit addled, poor creature. But harmless, I promise. And except for my Lizzie, he's still probably the brightest of the family."

"And her older brothers? The legal quartet? All four?"

"Three," Adam corrected. "Only three of them are lawyers."

"Here?"

"In the garden. Gin in hand."

"So soon," she said. "The thing is . . . I don't know what to come as."

"It's not a costume party."

"All dinner parties are," she said. "It's just that the costumes are usually habits. Uniforms. I have no uniform. Nothing feels at home on me. Lizzie will be in something simple but gorgeous, but she'll be wearing funky shoes or something, to show she doesn't take it too seriously. Her brothers will be in pastel oxford shirts and khaki pants; they'll be wearing ties to show they do take their outfits seriously, but summery ties with frogs or squirrels to show they know they're not at the office." She stepped back from poking around in the closet. "Oh God, Adam."

"Nome?"

"Promise me you won't take to wearing khaki pants just because . . . ," she teased.

"Not a chance," Adam swore. "I'm only marrying Lizzie, I'm not becoming a Barlow." He paused, then, "Nome, do you think I . . . ?"

Naomi went back in among her hanging clothes, still talking. "Lizzie's dad will have even tried to rumple himself, to loosen things up a bit, but he'll still seem all freshly pressed. They'll each be acting out their part. Even the children will be dressed as children. I hate my part." She backed out of the closet carrying a black dress: lace and fringes on the bodice and layers of black flounces down below.

"Do you think . . . ?" Adam tried again. "Am I making a mistake?"

Naomi left his question hanging in the air as she slipped into the black dress. "I could come as a flamenco dancer." She walked on tiptoe to the dresser and painted her lips in dark red. She angled her elbows, jutted her hips, stamped her bare heels on the floor. It was a strange little dance. The dress looked as though it wanted to be somewhere else. Naomi heel-struck across the room in a barefoot syncopation, then yanked the black costume over her head, throwing it to the floor, where it rippled and settled. "I guess you're wondering where I got all these."

Adam went to the window. "I keep telling myself"—he looked out on the garden down below, which was filled with his future in-laws—"it's not as though we'll be living with them."

Naomi now tied a long piece of red batik around her waist. "Look at this one. At least I can get it tight enough." Taking off her top, she draped a piece of orange silk around her neck, crossed it in front to cover her girlish breasts, then tied it in back. "What do you think?"

Adam was still looking out the window. "You know, sometimes I can't breathe. Lizzie is so much herself now, so distinct. But what if she turns into either one of her parents? I like to think that she and her twin, Hal, are foundlings, completely unrelated to the Barlows—that they were stolen from somewhere. But what if that's not true? Could I bear it if Lizzie turned into Philippa, or Stephen, or some mixture? I don't even know, sometimes—" Catching sight of Naomi in red and orange, Adam gave a quizzical look.

"What?" Naomi said. "What do you think? Too 'island princess'?" She laughed and undid the ties, tossing sarong and scarf on top of the rest of the discarded possibilities on the floor. She pulled on a black T-shirt printed with a large skull, in glossy black with a bit of silver. "You know, the first time I met Lizzie's dad—"

"You met Stephen Barlow?"

"Briefly. They came over for drinks one night before I left for Romania. You were off with Lizzie somewhere, I think in New York. I came in late; I'd been working at the hospice. Anyway, when I first met him, he asked me if I was a nun. Or some kind of missionary."

"What did you say?"

"I told them Jews don't really do either of those things. And that besides, I was an atheist."

"Nome. It's getting—"

"I know. Oh shit. My life is such a mess."

"Hey."

"I can't possibly come, you know."

"What are you talking about?"

"I'd be like the bad fairy."

"Couldn't you just come as, well, you know . . . ?"

"I'd jinx the whole thing. All I do is hang around with dead people, or people at grave risk." She gave a rueful smile, then said, "I feel like a mummy winder."

"A what?"

"The Egyptian person who winds the strips of gauze around mummies. Maybe an embalmer. Maybe that's what I am."

"Nome?"

"Every time I come home from somewhere, I think I'll never do it again. Then I stay home for a while and fatten up and get sane again—sort of—and work here with the dying, but I just can't settle here. I have to keep running away again. Maybe I should learn rugby. Wrestling."

"You have to weigh more than a hundred pounds for either one."

"I could become a cop," she joked. "I've seen featherweight cops. I'd have to grow my hair. . . . They always have ponytails, the lightweights, for gravitas."

"This is nuts. What's going on?"

"I really hate what I do."

"You mean, 'doing good'?"

"Good."

"Why do it, then? Why not get a job like normal people? Be a poet," he laughed. "Go to school."

"The problem is. Oh God, the problem, you see . . . Do you see the problem?"

"Not totally clearly."

"It's a question of the demons of pudding."

"Pudding?"

"Pudding. Cushiony things. Think of them as huge marshmallow pillows that come and suffocate me if I'm not careful. Those are my demons. If I don't do it, if I'm not in extremis, if I'm not in an apocalyptically unhygienic environment—trying to make things even a little better for others—I feel terminally bland. Silly and useless. Reprehensible. Without meaning."

"And when you *are* there? Surrounded by apocalypse?"

"Oh God," she laughed, then groaned. "It's so selfish of me to keep doing it because I'm not good at it, not at all. I get the terrors. I get rashes in the tropics. I get mosquito bites the size of tangerines. I can't sleep. Night noises appall me, but if the darkness is too quiet, I listen until I hyperventilate. Finally I get sick. I get so sick each time, I practically have to be medically evacuated. People end up taking care of me for longer than I was able to take care of anybody else."

"But when you're back here, working at hospice, it's okay, right?" Adam's voice was upbeat, hopeful, as though together they might both avoid desperation.

"Actually I do it because it's been the only way I can live with myself when I'm back here. I do it just until I get strong enough to go back to my latitudes of disaster. But I'm also terrible at working with the dying. I lark about and try to keep people amused, but I don't think someone as crazy as I am can be a good comforter. What I'm trying to say is that I'm almost as bad at hospice care as I am in the tropics. Volunteers confuse me with the dying ones. People who don't know that I'm on staff bring me food and try to get me to eat."

"Well, that makes a bit of sense, actually."

"Don't you start, too."

"Okay. But you do see the problem?"

"Of course I do. But I can't eat when I'm panicked. Or in love-catastrophe."

"Love! How does love come into it?"

"A fucking maelstrom. Every time. Why do you think I shaved my head in Bucharest?"

"I thought—we all thought—that it was head lice. From the orphanage."

"Not head lice. It was more like love rage. It felt like a good way to disentangle. He was one of the doctors. For a time he was so sweet. He would feed me cakes made of quinces, along with smoky tea. I even learned to cook for him: sausage meat in pickled cabbage leaves. Grilled meatballs with green herbs. Though it was his mother who made the little quince cakes, and she also pickled the cabbages. Hundreds of cabbages at a time. A universe of cabbages. When I'd been with him for about nine months, he decided to also take up with a village girl who had come to Bucharest from the Carpathian Mountains to make her living in the city. The oldest of problems. The oldest of professions. He wanted to save her. He kept asking me for small 'loans.' To him, all Americans were rich and undeserving, in equal measure. For some reason I accepted that view of things. When you're there long enough, you come to see things that way. But when he finally asked me to donate blood, because she needed some sort of transfusion, I knew it was time to save myself. I shaved my head and left him before he could give me any more of her little love diseases. Or bleed me dry. I was like the frog in the vat of slowly heating water. I neglected to jump out as soon as the pain of love surpassed the pleasure. Then it got so bad that I couldn't. God. Adam. It feels so good to be out of that. Finally I can sleep."

"Good. And can you eat?"

"Yes, I am beginning to. That has taken longer, somehow. But it is back, eating."

"As in dinner? Down in the garden?"

"Yes, now, down in the garden."

"Good."

"Adam?"

"Yeah?"

"Thanks for talking me down. Listen, will this black shirt be okay? Does the skull disturb you? Is it too visible? Do you mind if I wear black jeans?"

"A touch of goth. You're perfect. Come."

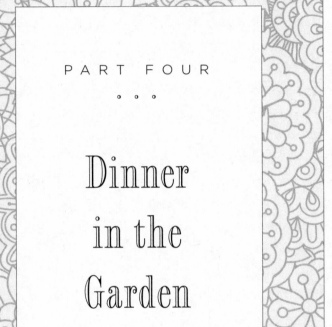

PART FOUR

. . .

Dinner in the Garden

Ah, Stephen," Celia called. "Come and sit. You are beside me, there." She felt incapable of talking with anyone and hoped that Stephen Barlow was prepared to show his social graces. She would listen to law, she would listen to heroic tales of golf, if only Naomi would come down from her room.

"Charlotte, you are over here, next to William. Where are the children? They sit at the other end. Liam next to Amy. Yes. Come. Sit. Barnes, you are between Sara and Olivia. William! On Philippa's left, over here." Celia wished she could sit beside Sara's priest. They could talk of plume poppies and the throats of daylilies and the strange properties of herbs. None of these Barlows seemed to have an eye for gardens. "Father Lombroso . . ."

"Dennis, please call me Dennis."

"Dennis, yes. Next to Sara, and also young Harriet."

SHE HAS SURROUNDED *me with Barlows,* thought Pindar. But it was childish to be upset, for the conjugal symmetries had also imprisoned Celia between father and grandfather of the bride, Judge Barlow on one side and wicked old Nathan Morrill on the other. Perhaps Celia had it worse than he did. On Pindar's other side was Larissa Barlow, married to one of the sons, but probably not to William Barlow, who sat just opposite him. All those sons. They would be gone before the night was over. It was just a matter of time.

Philippa Barlow spoke around him, now, addressing her daughter-in-law Larissa. "Such a delicious evening," she said. "I spent the day getting a new dishwasher. Why do machines always break down on the eve of a wedding?"

Pindar decided he didn't have to answer this. He wondered if there would be dancing at the wedding the next day, but he didn't really want to ask Philippa about it, even though she was in charge. She might think he was inviting her. He did love dancing, the combination of order and abandon. But he didn't want to talk about it with this woman he barely knew. He saw that this shyness would confine him to shallowness in all his dealings with her. And if there was dancing—would he have to take her, bronzed and bejeweled, in his arms? Would he have to allow Stephen Barlow to hold Celia, all of them caught in a web of social symmetries?

Pindar was light on his toes and heavy on his heels. When he walked barefoot, Celia told him she could hear his heels drumming on the hardwood floors—even when she was on the other side of the house. And yet at sixty, he still started each flight of stairs at a run. He and Celia were one of those older couples who looked totally ordinary and a bit dumpy standing still, but in motion it was as though they were demonstrating some new principle of physics, implying hidden systems and unsuspected harmonies. Dancing, they made the most intricate motions seem accessible and innate. This was not accomplished through acrobatic leaps or dips; rather they seemed grounded while moving, as though they were digging into or defining the earth, even as their movement seemed to reflect that of the planets. Like dervishes, their dance wasn't about speed; in fact, you couldn't tell whether it was slow or fast. You would wonder if their path had been inscribing letters or words on the dance floor, writing something that could be crucial to decipher and to know.

Borsuk stood just inside the kitchen door. "How do I look?" he said.

"Like a penguin, exactly," said Chhaya. "Where did you get a tuxedo? You are more elegant than them. Perhaps you will make Mr. Pindar feel ashamed."

"This is how waiters dressed in my country," he said. "In the old days, when everything counted."

"Then how did they tell the waiters from the others?"

"All are waiters," he said. "But only servers get to walk around. The others must sit there and eat what and when we please to bring them."

"Like animals?" Chhaya asked, smiling suddenly.

"Like pets," Borsuk answered. "It is up to us to teach them patience and behavior, like pets."

Chhaya nodded at him. "You look good," she said.

Naomi walked into the garden with Adam. Pindar got up and embraced his daughter. He could not keep himself from caressing her newly grown curls with his cupped hands, as he had done when she was a child. He always wanted to put Naomi's soul on some kind of a scale when he saw her, to measure her well-being. "Welcome," he whispered.

"I'm sorry to be so late. Getting dressed took hopelessly long."

Celia introduced Naomi and placed her between Charlotte

Morrill, the journalist, and young Harry Barlow. She was momentarily taken aback by Naomi's black outfit with the skull-bedecked T-shirt, but her happiness at her daughter's presence overcame any misgivings about her clothing and she expected that she would find it all humorous in the future. Besides, her girl looked lovely: Her face had healed; her cropped hair was growing into angelic auburn curls, and her frame, while still angular, no longer looked starved.

Pindar found that he could largely avoid talking if he kept asking questions of Philippa Barlow and appeared to listen to her responses. She didn't seem to be paying much attention to their conversation. He wondered if it was haze from the gin she had been drinking since she arrived, or if her mind was simply somewhere else. He himself was so inattentive, however, that several times he wondered which things he had already asked her and which he had only thought of asking, lining them up like peas in a row, ready to be flicked at a stone in the garden. As she chattered, Philippa reminded him of sparrows on a telephone wire, except that they chirped about important things like falling barometric pressure and the sweet possibility of rain. From time to time it seemed as though language had deserted him. He couldn't think of any topic in common with this woman with the California teeth and the gold bracelets. He couldn't think of any more questions to ask her.

Philippa turned to him. "Tennis?" she asked. "Which of you play?"

Pindar shook his head. "None of us, I'm afraid."

"Or golf perhaps?"

Pindar shook his head again, remembering to smile.

"Our older sons also play squash," she went on. "Stephen

used to play, but he's no longer as nimble as he once was. He really prefers golf."

"I see," said Pindar.

"Oh, but games! Surely you have some favorite games. Ping-Pong?" Philippa saw from his quizzical look that Pindar didn't have any favorite games. "But don't you miss the thrill of it all?" She would certainly miss it. She played tennis almost every weekday and loved the rules, the seesawing of points, the handsome darting about, even the sweat. She sometimes joined Stephen on the golf course, but never with the craving and exultation that came over her with tennis. She loved winning but also loved the fact that someone would eventually win, even if it wasn't her. To her the game stood for something much larger than a small fur-covered sphere of rubber walloped over a boundary of knotted string, though she wasn't sure what exactly. She could not understand how anyone would be immune to its exhilaration. Not to know tennis seemed like such a shame. She wondered if she should offer to teach him. Or would that seem too patronizing? Of course, he might prefer sedentary games. "Bridge?" she offered. "Poker?" Nothing. "What about chess?"

Pindar brightened. "Ah, chess," he said. "We taught the children when they were little, and Adam and Sara played on their own for a bit. They taught themselves Go, but then, you know, it turned out they both preferred to read."

"Monopoly?"

"Ah, yes," Pindar said. "We all played Monopoly together for a time, in the summers mostly, but it sort of faded. The children said they were not so interested in real estate."

"Ah, children," Philippa said. "One worries about them so."

She kept her graveled voice low because she didn't want Larissa, seated on Pindar's other side, to hear. Philippa knew there was some critical torque in her son Barnes's marriage. Barnes did not exhibit any of the smug entitlement of his adulterous brother William. It was more likely that someone had been finding the brittle Larissa attractive.

"Excuse me?" Pindar had been woolgathering.

"Yes, yes," Philippa Barlow was saying, more insistently this time. She could see that Pindar was not connecting to what she was asking. She repeated it: "Don't you worry about your children?" She nodded at Sara, who was just now running across the grass to take her place at the table beside the priest.

"Worry?" Pindar said this as though it would never have occurred to him. He had no intention of telling Philippa Barlow about his experiences with his daughters. Mrs. Barlow's feelings about her fair-haired hulking lawyer sons had nothing to do with that mix of silk and bird bone—in airports, orphanages, asylums, supermarkets—that was Naomi, nor the cohabiting with scorpions and with the spiritual that was his daughter Sara.

As Philippa looked at him with her sociably painted lips and her powdery descending jowls, Pindar pulled himself up straight, pressing his spine to the back of his chair so hard that his innards ached. "But what have you got to worry about?" he said, gesturing around the table with his wineglass as though he were toasting her sons in their light-colored shirts. "They are suffused with success, your brood."

"OH. ANOTHER BAT," said Stephen Barlow. "Why do they keep coming down here? Are you frightened? Shall I chase him away?"

"Not at all," replied Celia. "I love them. They are so hard to parse. They have a roost somewhere nearby. They have always been here."

LOOKING AT NAOMI opposite him, Cameron could see that she was burning. He couldn't tell if it was a sort of self-ignited state, or from something external to herself. She seemed part gamine, part waif. He longed to touch her hair, her slender arms, and he found her black T-shirt immeasurably daring and funny. She was so different from all the Barlow women, who seemed to enter any new setting waving flags of their own competence and abilities ahead of them. This one needed to be taken care of, and he found himself yearning to do it. His own face had grown hot from watching her. He looked around to see if anyone had noticed. Far down the table his wife, Amy, was deep in talk with Naomi's sister and the Jesuit. Everyone was elsewhere in their gaze. He looked at Naomi. "Who are you?" he said.

"I am Naomi," she laughed. "We've just been introduced."

"Yes, but who really?" Then he felt himself blushing even more.

THE END OF the clear brilliant summer day, cloudless, perfect but for a grievous crack in the blue made by a single contrail. Was it grief, or fear of grief? Pindar tried to look around the scar, at the whole beauty of what was left. Something was eluding him. He could feel it slipping through his fingers, escaping from focus like floaters in the eye. If he could only hold on to it. But grasping it would be like netting motes in a beam of sunlight: If the sieve was fine enough, it wouldn't swing through the air fast enough to catch anything. He often had this feeling when driving home. As his car came to the turn for his street at the top of the hill, it felt as though meaning was about to be disclosed to him at exactly this point in space; all was about to become clear, everything! Clear enough to taste with his mind, and swallow. But always he veered off, his car and his attention, turning in to the street of his home. It wasn't that his home was in the way of meaning, it was that somehow he always managed to skitter off, looking away just when the one thing that mattered was about to reveal itself. He felt that now, sitting beside Philippa Barlow, and he felt furthermore that if he didn't catch it now, whatever it was, then he never would, and his life would be at best a gentle letdown, a descent along the known path where he now existed. What if this dinner party was not an interruption *in* his work, but *was* the work itself? What if the secret lay here, at this table, even beside this chattering woman, mother of the bride? What if the secret was darting above him, zigzagging, waiting to be noticed and plucked from the sky?

Philippa Barlow broke in. "I am tormented by household appliances," she said. "Usually they wait until August to go on the blink, but this year they have started already, and it is only June. What is the quietest vacuum cleaner, do you think?"

As SARA SAT down beside Dennis, she looked around at the seated families. With the oblique angle of the lowering sun, the white tablecloths appeared fringed with lightning. Ripples in the air surrounded her father's head as he stood to pour wine, and sparks licked at her mother's silver hair.

The flowers in their brass vases heaved and beckoned. Goatsbeard and Queen Anne's lace; Black-eyed Susan and Jacob's ladder. Dennis asked Sara who had arranged them.

"My dad," she said. "Why?"

"He has paired the sexes, mixed royalty with commoners, Jews with Gentiles and perhaps even with heathens, if you think of the goatsbeard as Pan."

"Oh," she said. "I didn't know anyone would notice."

His fingers brushed her arm.

PINDAR PULLED ALL his body so straight that it seemed to freeze around his spine; he scowled with the physical effort.

"Are you all right? Is there something the matter?"

"No, no, a spasm. The back. We were carrying tables earlier." He gave a bit of a grimace. "I'm afraid I don't know too much about vacuums." His eyes ached from looking at the sky. He didn't want to tell her anything. Something was waiting for him to grasp it, more visible than usual. But how could he do it when he had such a pain in his forehead, when his back twinged whenever he was imprudent enough to forget its existence, when he had such a yearning for his pipe and for a cup of coffee? Beset by small bothers. Wouldn't it be better to wait until the guests had gone home and his medieval carcass was calmer and all its wants had been satisfied? He saw that this was like saying, *I'm feeling a bit off right now, and I have to sit here at this dinner party, so I guess I can't go looking for the absolute.* His objections were nonsense. He would get to the bottom of it this very time. That was the purpose of this dinner party. Of course, everyone else thought the party was in order to knit the Cohen and Barlow clans together, for Adam and Eliza's sake. He kept forgetting this, kept wandering off into his own universe. But the heart of the matter must be in both places, in the sociability of the dinner and in his own dark grapplings with attention. For that was what it would take, he saw, a staying of the gaze. A not veering away from looking at the light, was that it? Or was it the darkness that he was supposed to be looking at? He didn't know what texts could help him here. The whole question reminded him of reading Ezekiel, and how his mind always took off on a tangent instead of staring straight ahead until he understood it. Until he could picture the geometry and meaning of the wheels and flames and eyes. The quartet of angels he could see. He had even constructed them, making them out of gingerbread, each winter. They would stand, notched and interlocking, about a foot high. But the "wheels within wheels" that Ezekiel spoke of eluded him; they seemed impossible to construct and bake out of cookie dough. Was he really supposed to understand the vision of some exiled mystical prophet? Or was he supposed to have his own crazed vision? What did he mean by "supposed," anyway? Who had set up the rules here? How could he figure all this out in the middle of a dinner party when he was supposed to be taking care of his guests and talking about vacuum cleaners?

Pindar lifted the bottle of white wine and turned to Philippa Barlow. "More wine for you?"

SARA COULD SEE that Stephen Barlow was arguing with her mother and that Amy Barlow was talking to her little boy, Liam. Taking a deep breath she leaned toward Dennis. "So here we are," she said in a low, steady voice. "Face-to-face. Or side to side. Close enough. I think you and I have been thinking along the same lines." She wasn't going to let him be the first to break up; it was to be a tie.

"Truly?"

"Yes, I think we have converged."

"Oh. Then you don't mind my bringing it up?"

"Not at all."

"It will be vastly different," he said. Then, smiling, "But I'm sure you can handle it."

Sara looked at him. Why was he getting happier while she was getting sadder? "Yes," she said. "We both can."

"A huge change," he said.

"Change can be illuminating."

"And you're quite ready?"

"If you are." She tried to sound jaunty. Why did he want to break up in front of all these people? Shouldn't they be alone to do this? What if she fell apart?

"You know how important it all is to me." He looked down, grinning as he smoothed the tablecloth with his palms.

"And to me, too."

"It will make us even closer, I think."

"Closer?" Sara croaked. Her throat had closed up and she could barely talk. Perhaps she was turning into a frog. That was what grief did to the unwary.

"I know. It's hard to think of us being any closer. We will see each other in a new light."

Across the table Celia had been noting the intensity of this conversation, though she couldn't hear it because they were speaking so softly. To cut it short, she said, "Sara, sweetheart, could you help your father with the wine?"

Sara gestured to Celia, gave a broad smile. How did her mother always know when somebody needed saving? Still smiling, she pulled back her chair. "Don't go anywhere," she said to Dennis. "I'll be back in a moment."

GRACE DANE MAZUR

• • •

Philippa held her glass out to Pindar. "Thank you. Wonderfully cold, this white," she said. "Of course, refrigerators are harassing me as well. I'm planning to design one with no depth at all, so nothing can get lost at the back." What could she talk to this man about? She was running out of appliances. She didn't dare ask him about books. He might answer. She didn't feel she could talk to him about her work. She loved her work. Most of her clients were at a happy point in their lives where they had enough goods and dollars and now they wanted to give to those who would live after them. And they had enough money to pay for lawyers who could prevent, as much as possible, anything falling through the cracks between the outstretched hands of the generations.

Occasionally Philippa's clients showed up in a state of resentful exclusionism: "I don't want James to get one red cent! I do not even want him mentioned in my will." Or they would mention James but leave him a derisory sum. And she did have one adamant Boston dowager try to leave only a silver thimble to her least favorite daughter. Philippa had wondered at that point if she and the dowager had fallen into some sort of fairy tale, in which case the thimble would turn out to be worth more than the rest of the estate, which was to be divided among the rest of the heirs in a somewhat thoughtless manner. But such whimsy was rare, and mostly it was the joy of providing down the ladder, stretching from extreme old age to newborns and future-borns, these lines of forward-looking filiation.

Recently Philippa had been wishing she knew some way to provide for the emotional well-being of successive generations—if only she could write *that* into her wills. She looked down the table: All her children looked miserable except for Harry and Eliza. What was wrong with them all? She didn't know if it was true that William was leading a parallel life in Paris, but Olivia looked so sad that Philippa's heart went out to her. Cam and Amy had been fine, though she hoped Amy was unaware of what Cam was presently doing at the table. And poor Barnes had withdrawn into himself—Philippa knew, without her grand-daughter Harriet having told her, that Barnes and Larissa had been snarling at each other for weeks now. She wondered if this was partly her fault.

Philippa had tried to do something about Larissa. The girl had flair and brains but no calling except for a certain elegance. Finding a suitable charity for Larissa to give her time and energies to had not been easy. The young woman wanted nothing to do with illness or death. Hospitals were out, even the gardens at Mount Auburn Cemetery were too linked to mortality. Adult literacy had not been a good match, for Larissa had felt no kinship to grown-ups who couldn't read. In short, she needed a charity for people who didn't need charity: the wealthy and/or the immortal. Or at least the youthful. The symphony and the opera didn't quite fit, as she wasn't at all fond of music, but the museums with their galas would be perfect. Philippa had been sure that Larissa would flourish in some gallant committee at the Museum of Fine Arts. That had worked, and Philippa had taken great pride, until Larissa had veered slightly and fallen in love with the extraordinary Japanese collection there. Now she wanted to become a docent. The training program was proving difficult to get into, even though she had majored in art history at Smith, but the girl was showing a sudden doggedness and had taken up studying Japanese. This was so unlike her, this intellectual interest and tenacity, that Philippa had begun to suspect the existence of a beautiful Japanese gentleman somewhere in the picture, which might account, she thought, for the rockiness of the marriage.

WHY DID THE edge of clarity always present itself to him at such muddled times? Pindar wondered. He was reminded of the strange feeling he had on waking from his nap as the dark-haired child was tugging his foot: that all things were suddenly accessible. It wasn't a question of attaining some lonely prom-ontory on the coast and looking out at a small boat, solitary and lost on the vast empty reach of the sea—the alone with the alone. No, it was here, this very night, in the middle of the to-gether. This dinner party would be his vehicle; this evening's time would not be wasted.

Pindar glanced at Philippa and then away so as not to seem to be inspecting her. She was not an unattractive woman, and there were faint signs in her of the girl she had once been. She was not beautiful, though she carried herself as though she thought she was now and always had been. He wondered what would happen if he put his hand on her thigh under the table-cloth. Instead, he sipped some water and wondered at his silli-ness. But now, as though someone had read his mind, something was rubbing his foot. He choked on his drink. Something was lurking there by his foot, ready to rub again. He paused, stopped coughing, drank more water. At least it wasn't Philippa, unless she was hopelessly agile and long-legged, as it was his foot on Issa Barlow's side that had received the attention. Of course, it might have been the cat. He listened for purring, but there was too much dinner party chatter. Then he burst out, "Do you think that intelligence is connected to beauty?"

Across from Pindar, William Barlow said, "I've always found that the loveliness of the Parisian women—"

Philippa broke in. "That is clothing, not beauty."

Her voice had been unnecessarily sharp, Pindar thought. Hoping to mollify both sides, he said, "They do take such pains, the Parisian women. They have all the trappings of seduction. But I wonder if perhaps beauty is something else."

Philippa laughed, showing many teeth. She was nervous and didn't know if Pindar was being ironic about intelligence and beauty. She still thought it odd that the Cohens had chosen to eat in the garden when there was a large enough dining room indoors. Mosquitoes would come, and things with too many legs. The bats were already perilous. Strains of music came from beyond the woods. There was that other party going on up the road. She had seen those guests getting out of their cars when she and Stephen had overshot the Cohens' driveway trying to find the house. Those other guests had seemed deft and elegant. Here at this homely and awkward rehearsal dinner she felt, as always, shunted off to the margins of social life, aware of but not present at the glamorous excitement a few doors away. Which tonight had a live jazz band. That was so romantic that it tore at her heart.

Pindar watched Philippa as she laughed. How different she seemed from her daughter, Eliza, who was still a comforting flaxen beauty. One day, of course, Eliza would wake up and find that her mother's face had usurped her own and would gasp and call out that there had been some mistake. With Adam it would be the same, only he would find Pindar there instead of himself. The law of generations was ironclad. Pindar himself had turned into the father he had never known very well, who had appeared and disappeared at disconcerting intervals. Gabriel Cohen had sent his blessings for the wedding but claimed to be too infirm to travel. He would be in his nineties now. Pindar's favorite picture of him showed Gabriel in his mid-sixties, bearded and slightly stooped, standing in a garden outside of Paris. Pindar himself had never been as dapper or elegant as his father appeared in that picture from Bures-sur-Yvette, but their posture was nearly identical—the same sloped shoulders and forward-peering head—though Gabriel's beard was more pointy. Their resemblance was almost enough to make one doubt mortality.

Philippa was touching Pindar's arm to get his attention.

"Speaking of beauty," Philippa said. "Your mother must have been irresistible in her day." She nodded toward Leah.

In the middle of the long table, Leah was talking with Philippa Barlow's father, Nathan Morrill. Pindar watched them and hoped that Philippa hadn't noticed that the pair were flirting.

Leah had warned Pindar before the party began. "Now, don't go seating me next to some stain-shirted dotard, just because we're both old," she said. "There will be trouble if you do that. There will be spitting and clawing." She told him to remember back to when she had made him play with some other little boy simply because they were the same age and because she was having tea with the boy's mother. How he had despised those afternoons. The other boy was always sportive. While the mothers ate curious pale delicacies consumed only at teatime, ghosts of real food, Pindar would have to go outdoors and experience the humiliation of sticks and balls.

"Remember how bitterly you complained?" Leah said. "Well, it's even worse at this end of one's mortal career: 'Darling old lady, you must meet my palsied droopy-lipped grandparents, my dead auntie. You will love them.' It's like being in a stable with strange old cows, all wild eyes and smells and halting ruminations. Makes one want to commit violence."

Later, Pindar had laughed when he saw that Celia planned to seat his mother beside Mrs. Barlow's antique father—rumored to be mentally distant. Sweet payback for all his childhood play afternoons, he thought. But he did beg Celia to put the beautiful young Harry Barlow on Leah's other side, to compensate for the geezer. Harry was the only male Barlow with any real physical beauty, or any mischief in his soul. Where had they stolen him from?

Pindar saw that he had to figure everything out right then, while Philippa was speaking to him. For what if Death came and grabbed his arm instead of Philippa Barlow? Shanghaied him and pulled him away to where he would no longer be capable of doing his work. Dread flowed through him, making each vein a thoroughfare of consciousness. The bats darting overhead no longer looked like helpful and comical fruit eaters; they were dark little ideas, too quick to catch. He wanted to throw something at them. He saw, too, that he couldn't jettison his conversation with Philippa, sitting there beside him only because of the marriage of their offspring—he could not even slight her but would have to concentrate on her as well as on the thing that mattered, the nature of time. This other activity would have to remain invisible to Philippa, to everyone. He would have to pay attention to everything, even the dinner party, which with its snorts and wheezing and sudden laughter reminded him of the sounds a sea serpent might make when surfacing in a warm ocean—its head over there, ready to jump into the unknown upper world and grasp and comprehend the universe; its tail over there, where the young children were sitting, ready to follow wherever the foreparts might lead, leaving in the end its wake traveling behind.

"Do you think that my father is flirting with your mother?" broke in Philippa.

"Excuse me?" said Pindar.

"The old ones—flirting?" Philippa gestured discreetly.

"Oh," said Pindar, as though he had not noticed this. He realized that he had been thinking of his conversation with Philippa as an interruption. But that would only be true if time were linear, a single line with a unique direction. Which was absurd. The arrow wasn't even the proper shape to denote distance. We tend, he thought, to consider distance as though we had nothing but a yardstick or a string and a stone to measure it with, but we experience it as some sort of sprouting and folding and buckling. When we distill it to a single dimension in order to describe it by measurement, we lose the whole richness and feeling of distance.

He looked now in the direction of Philippa's gesture. "Oh," he said again. "Our parents. Do you think so?"

PHILIPPA'S NEW SANDALS pinched a little. No one would notice if she slipped them off for a while. There. Of course she had gotten new shoes and new jewelry for tonight's dinner as well as for the wedding. There was a ritual need for such purchases, as well as a ritual joy. She had realized as she and Stephen were on the way here—and she wasn't sure why it had taken her fifty-nine years to see this—that women were really dressing for other women. Men didn't notice, in her experience, or if they did, they only noticed what women's clothing had left uncovered—

cleavage, neck, arms, legs—while women's perceptions were so finely tuned to the coverings. Women could place a dress, by catalog or designer; they knew how much it cost as well as what fiber or mix of fibers it was made of. More than that, they knew how it would feel on the body, how itchy or soothing, how constricting or wallowy. And the moment they could *not* place something—even a shoe, an earring, a handbag—it bothered them and they would shower the wearer with compliments until she proudly, and perhaps a bit ruefully, let slip some clue as to where she had purchased it.

This was not to say that women didn't dress to attract men, or to make an impression on them, but it was the women who *understood* what other women wore, while the men simply *reacted*.

In her own family, Philippa knew that tonight it was only her sister, Charlotte, who noticed and understood. Eliza might sometimes notice but didn't understand much about clothing; she really cared more about cows. And tonight she was too busy being a bride. Philippa's daughters-in-law rarely commented on what she wore. Perhaps they didn't dare; she didn't know. Of the Cohen women, only Mrs. Leah Cohen had properly inspected her, but then Leah was so old, it probably didn't matter. As for the others, Celia was busy hosting this whole gathering, Sara was too involved with her Jesuit, and Naomi, in her black outfit with the silver-sequined skull, well, Philippa would just as soon *not* be noticed by Naomi.

But it wasn't as though her efforts had been for nothing. The delicious strappy sandals—a bit girlish, but so what—and her bracelets and necklace with the gold wire and quartz stones, these kept her going. But more than that: What the women wore for one another bolstered them all. It defined civilization. If that was too strong, say rather that it gave them all a certain form of courage. And the men, well, even if they never really saw, and didn't have the language to capture or discuss, they too must feel, on some not quite conscious level, the atmosphere created by the women, and were buoyed or carried along by it. She supposed that something similar could be said for the men, though she doubted their pleasure was as intense and suspected that the courage they got from their clothing was more like that of armor or uniform.

PINDAR TURNED HIS thoughts back to time. What exactly was a moment? Was it the shortest span of time that could be represented by art? Perhaps moments were like sheets of gold leaf, hammered ever so thin, each leaf the locus for new thoughts. Time would then be a matter of layering, so that each second had a stack of moments on top, a baklava of time. Was this why his new Babylonian fragment had the word *layers,* then a gap where a piece was chipped out, then *time*? Or was that word *branches* rather than layers? Perhaps time wasn't flat after all. In that case, no sheaves like baklava, but filaments like kataifi, those nests made of shredded pastry drenched with syrup or honey. He saw the pastry threads as silver, now, each strand branching into new trees of silvery time growing out from each second, all of them inhabited by breath. For breathing had become necessary to his conception of time, inspiration and expiration. He needed the gods to breathe into him, breathe through him like a flute.

"YOU WERE A good *what*?" asked Leah Cohen.

Nathan Morrill leaned toward Leah with his whole body because it no longer bent in parts. "A chef," he said. "Not half-bad. Amazing, actually. Now I have these," he said, looking down at his hands. He lifted his left hand and put it on Leah's arm. It felt like a skillet, a kettle full of water.

"Tell me a dish."

"Since we are eating this asparagus, I will tell you an hors d'oeuvre, a finger food, which needs to be made carefully." He looked down at his own fingers and tried to splay them. "Consider a large basil leaf, of the immense variety whose name I forget; now consider a small rectangle of fontina cheese on it, and on top of that a similar rectangle of Bosc pear. Finally you wrap the basil leaf around pear and cheese and, using a thread you have pulled from a cooked leek, you tie it all up into a neat little package."

"Leek? Why not use chives to tie your packet?"

"Chives are never as strong as they look."

As she made the rounds of the table with her bottles of wine, Sara knew it was silly to keep trying to see the dinner table itself as a scorpion, with all of its articulations and repeated segments, all those appendages hidden under the tablecloth. The image didn't really work. For one thing, there were too many legs underneath. Forty-six, not counting Shamhat the cat—if that was who had been rubbing her foot. Perhaps Philippa Barlow at one end of the table was really the stinger, though she did not seem all that powerful or poisonous. Then the children at the other end would be the claws, the pedipalps, clawing their way into the future. But the children's end of the table wasn't even symmetric, with the empty place her mother had set for some forgotten latecomer or prophet. It didn't work, her scorpion image, but she couldn't entirely get it out of her head. The enlivened dinner table must have a better analogue in the world of jointy-legged animals. Perhaps the silkworm, then, for it did after all spin things: conversations, narratives, connections, entangle-ments.

Sara sat down again beside Dennis. She made herself sit straight and tall as though nothing terrible had happened. She exhaled. "How should we do it? Do you think we should have one last dinner, one last evening together? Or should this party be the last one?"

"One last dinner? With your family, you mean?"

"No no." Why on earth would they want her beloved fam-ily? "Just you and me."

"But, love, you and I should have very many dinners, an in-finity of evenings."

"Won't that make it too hard?" She looked away from him, sadder than she could imagine. How had she thought she would know how to break up with this man? Where would she direct each new thought? Who would hold the other end of each strand? She could practically hear the sizzle and hiss as things fell into the void.

"LIZ," HARRY WHISPERED to his twin. "Don't worry. I can marry you two right here, under full cover of company. The whole ceremony, right now, in no time at all. If we keep our voices soft and our gestures toward the food. Are you ready?" He drank some wine and motioned to Eliza and Adam to do the same. "Weddings are very old," he began in a conversational voice. "We were doing them before we swung down out of the trees and figured out how to stand upright. Rituals of fertility, planting, seasons, property, and clan alliances—all of these have ended up in a ceremony that is so old there may never have been a time when the participants actually understood the words. Each civilization also weaves in its own strands of current meaning. Harry poured a little of his wine on the ground, then said, "Adam, a poem?"

Adam lifted his wineglass to Eliza, and began reciting softly, one of his poems. But soon he forgot to whisper and the whole table grew quiet. Even the children looked up, startled.

Listening to her son, Celia wondered where his poetry came from. He was not the howling sort. Part of his wildness came from his delight in words, their music, the sparks as they collided. But it seemed to come also from some further place, down where presence was laced with loss, and beauty danced with grief. She often wondered if she and Pindar were less deep than their three offspring. She at any rate. These were among the things she could not ask. She felt a lack. An envy.

Across the table from Adam, old Leah Cohen caught her grandson's eye and lifted her glass to him. She hoped he would tell his poems all night.

WATCHING ADAM, STEPHEN Barlow felt pity for Celia. Clearly, Barlow felt, the boy had some sort of disability that took the form of his not being able to see and express things in clear. He would never make it in the real world. As the young man recited, the disjunction of poets and golf presented itself to Stephen Barlow: Why was it that poets were not found on the links? Was it simple physical ineptitude? Did their legs wobble? Were their backs askew? Or did they not *need* golf? Could they be beyond it?

• • •

"WATER?" NAOMI ASKED Cameron. "Are you as parched as I am?" She and Cameron gazed at each other and neither of them could seem to let go.

Cameron burned in response to Naomi. He was as parched as she was. As they sat across the table from each other, whenever the space between them was violated by the passing of a dish, a word, a glance from one of the others, they each gave an almost imperceptible frown.

Pindar looked over at his daughter: Naomi was keyed up tonight, inflamed. He didn't know if he had to save her. Or even if he could. Naomi was usually attracted to sinkholes of danger, the ones with only a dark hollow at the core, but this young Barlow looked smart and kind and benign. Of course! He was married. That was the danger here.

PINDAR WAS USED to working with gaps. The ancient clay tablets inscribed with his Babylonian recipes were almost always broken, even when they had been kiln-fired. He was used to ambiguities and loved fitting them together. The most famous texts from ancient Mesopotamia had the great blessing of redundancy: Apprentice scribes were given the task of copying all the important works as a way to learn their craft, so there were multiple copies of the epic of Gilgamesh, for example. Naturally these copies were also broken, but in random places, so that a coherent text could often be cobbled together. Then, too, the ancient poems were full of repeats and refrains, making it easy to guess at what was missing. The old recipes that Pindar studied, however, had not been used for copy practice, and recipes have no refrains. They were singular and rare. What was missing was lost.

His old thought-demons approached now, trying to lure him away with reason. This was not rational, they said, to picture crucial things like time in terms of honey-soaked Middle Eastern pastries. It was foolish to seek illumination in the middle of a dinner party. He was supposed to get his son, Adam, married. Be reasonable, his demons said. Work for communal blessing, and put off this selfish and dicey search until the guests are gone, your desk is clean, your mind uncluttered, and your memory clear.

But what if he should die? That was the flaming weapon he shook at the demons he called Holding Back and Sloth. They always came in pairs or quartets, his demons. He could almost see them: They had multiple wings and bore the heads of men and oxen, eagles and lions. They told him he should not expect to figure anything out during a party. Revelation, he replied, was never an act of reason. At this they bowed, slightly, all four of them, linked at the tips of their wings, then twisting like smoke they backed away.

So Pindar would do it now. He would slip seconds made of lapis lazuli among the beaten golden sheets of time. He would do it while sitting next to Philippa Barlow, listening to her talk about refrigerators, about Ping-Pong and tennis, and if he got anywhere, if he untangled any of the knots, then he would always link his findings with Philippa, simply because she had been at his side when he did this, due to the conjugal patterns of this gathering, and by being there, then, she would achieve and deserve a place in his mind, a bit horrible but necessary, and he would have to feel for her a sort of love.

• • •

HARRY TURNED TO Adam. "Do you want some asparagus?" he said. And privately, "And are you *willing*? Seriously and now?"

"I am," said Adam.

"Liz?"

"Yes, please pass it. I am willing, seriously and now, and even if we get interrupted."

As she listened to Harry and the bridal pair, Leah turned to Nathan Morrill. "Are you still a serious cook?" she said.

"Not really," Nat Morrill said, yawning and putting a heavy hand to his mouth. "Sorry. About these yawns, I mean. They are not in my control. As for cooking: I can barely manage. My daughter Philippa threatens me with one of those microwave ovens. I tell her that if she gives me one I shall put my head in it. I have a Polish friend in Paris who eats only raw things. I would rather do that than use a microwave, which is not cooking as we know it, but something else: I think it simply bothers the molecules of things until they give up and become soft. I, for one, refuse to do it." His head lowered to his chest.

"Heads up, Leah," whispered Adam. "Stop flirting and uphold what we are doing."

"I am not flirting. My head is erect, although my elderly dinner partner is taking his pre-post-prandial snooze. So I am watching you and drinking to you, in the name of all that is holy and much that is not."

NATHAN MORRILL WAS dozing. He had dozed off in the middle of saying something to Leah; his head had simply slipped down until his jaw rested on his chest, his slack mouth softly hissing. Pindar, watching him, felt waves of tiredness in his own back.

He reached for the wine and poured more for Philippa on one side, and for Issa Barlow on the other, then finally for himself.

"WHAT? DID YOU speak?" Startled, shattered, Cameron couldn't tell if Naomi was making an offer or a command.

"Water?" Naomi repeated. "I was feeling a bit . . . and just wondering if you wanted—"

"I," he said. Then, "You are very kind to ask."

She poured his water. "More asparagus?"

"Please." He let her serve him and then he passed the platter to his brother Babar's wife, Issa, on his left. Turning back to Naomi he said, *"Exquisite creatures who had been pleased to assume vegetable form."*

"What?" Naomi said.

"Proust," Cam replied. "He says they have an iridescence that is not of this world." He blushed. This was not the kind of conversation he would dare attempt among Barlows.

"I'm lost. Who has?"

"Asparagus. Stalks of asparagus."

"Oh," Naomi said. "I didn't know he wrote about such things. But I'm the only one of my family who has never read him."

"That's fine," Cam said. "I'm the only one in my family who has."

"These don't look so iridescent." She dangled a spear on the end of her fork. "Does he mean purple ones? White?"

DOWN AT THE other end of the table, seven-year-old Liam said, "I don't like this stuff." He poked at the green stalks on his plate. "Let's go find fish."

"Where?" asked Emily, leaning her elbows on the table. She was eight and ready for anything.

"In the pond."

Three-year-old Eli looked up from the green things he had been mashing on his plate. He grunted a happy assent.

"Well, we'll have to be careful," said Laurie, who was ten. "I happen to know for a fact that half of the frogs in that pond are poisonous. Besides, they'll never let us leave this table."

"We could do it silently," said Harriet, the other ten-year-old. "We won't tell them. If we just dribble away, one by one, they'll never notice we've gone."

"WELL THEN," HARRY said quietly. His cheeks reddened. If he could only get it right this time. He had performed six other marriages, four of which dissolved within months. Harry had taken these failures personally and thought that perhaps they had been caused by his own imperfect knowledge. There was some wording of the spells that would bind his sister to Adam and not let them come undone. One of his past grooms had telephoned him every night for three months, howling his rage at his ex-love, as though Harry had been to blame. And of course Harry felt at fault. He grieved for his friends but also for his own obvious incompetence. Two of his couples had asked for annulments. He didn't do annulments. Go back to your Catholics, he told them. One of his friends had challenged him to find a good *unbinding* ritual to serve instead of an annulment. What you can do, the friend insisted, you must learn to undo. But Harry hadn't found such a ceremony yet. It would have to be vehement and terrifying, and bring, in the end, something close to serenity, some sort of forgiveness for mistaken love. Exorcism of a failed marriage was still beyond his powers.

"Hal," Eliza whispered. She knew that her twin's long silences sometimes had to be interrupted. "Come back to us. You were saying?"

"Sorry," Harry said. "Adam: going back to our earlier conversation. People are really difficult to take care of. Worse than pets. Harder than poems. Take this woman, for example." He gestured to his twin.

"Oh yes. I take you, Eliza," said Adam.

Naomi looked over at her brother. She caught Adam's eye. *I see that you are up to something, though I don't know what it is. I have no attention to spare; I cannot detach myself yet from Cameron, who sits across from me and whom I have just met and fallen into.* She kissed the rim of her wineglass, and blew across it to Adam and then to Eliza. Then she gave back to Cameron, older brother of the bride, her jealous gaze.

OF COURSE, THERE was a further problem, and Pindar couldn't tell if this was his reason speaking, or his demons, for sometimes they mirrored each other. How could he decipher time when he was so embedded in it? Seeing anything deeply involves a stepping back. To be a philosopher of food, one could not be in the throes of eating. To work on the aesthetics of sex, one could not be in flagrante. In looking at art, one could not be in the midst of painting it. In psychotherapy, one tried to stop feeling a bit, or to step back and gaze at the self while it was feeling, in order to comb for patterns, interruptions, dislocations. One had to draw oneself in a little, in order to get a broader view—

and yet the passions might be, must be, still hot. This art of stepping back, when one yearned so to be right in the midst, this took some learning.

AMY LOOKED UP and down the table. At least the kids were behaving. Her daughter, Emily, was doing something with some sort of insect, offering it water from a spoon. Liam was cutting his asparagus, though Amy knew he had no intention of eating it. But Cam! He was practically falling into the younger Cohen girl's plate. Naomi, that was her name. She couldn't be more than twenty-three or twenty-four. What was he thinking? Cam was a dear, and particularly wonderful when compared with his brothers, Harry-the-mystic, Babar-the-silent with his not entirely faithful Issa, and William-the-entitled with his poor sad Olivia.

Amy had recently started taking Olivia to lunch to try to cheer her up. Sometimes she got Issa to join them, but Issa diverted all conversations to herself and how attractive she found Japanese men. Finally one day when Amy and Olivia were alone, Olivia had asked her, "Is it better to be married to someone who is only half with you, or is it better to not be married at all and to raise your kids alone?"

"Do you mean, because he's only home half the time? Or because of his involvement with war crimes?"

"Ah. War crimes. Nothing at home can ever be as crucially important as war crimes. I do understand that. But I meant, someone whose *heart* is only half with me," Olivia said. "He has a Parisian someone."

Amy was proud of herself for realizing that she had no idea how to answer. She finally said, "Are you lonely when he's home with you? Or are you just lonely when he's gone?"

"I don't know," Olivia said, crumpling.

During those lunches Amy had always felt so secure with her Cam. She thought of herself and Cam as the peaceful ones in the family, and she knew that that was how the elder Barlows thought of them. But perhaps being the happiest couple was a position of danger, from which one could be toppled at any moment. Look at him over there. He must be talking about books, Proust probably—his cheeks were so red. Perhaps Olivia and Issa would soon be taking *her* to lunch, but she didn't think so. She and Cam enjoyed each other so much, even though they'd been together for a decade. Just being with each other made the darkest nights pass and each glorious dawn arrive.

"Sorry," said Nat Morrill, flailing. His wineglass rocked; he caught it. "Snoozing is so impolite. I cannot control it. I get clobbered with fatigue at the oddest times. I do not know if it comes from the Lyme disease or if it is some private failure of the will. Which is what I suspect. Where were we?"

"You were telling me of your friend who eats all things without cooking."

"Bless you for remembering. That is correct. Without cooking *and* without mixing. No salt, except alone, in a course by itself, called 'salt.' "

"Raw? Even meat?"

"Meat, too, she keeps away from fire, and from mixtures. It is better to keep things pure, she says."

"And keep her," Harry said to Adam. He wondered why marriage was so much more mysterious to him than to each of the couples he had consecrated. They'd seemed to waltz right into it, or rather tango right in—for what they did was dashing and romantic, with much twining of bodies and twisting of heads. They never realized that people are really trees, whose roots need to grow into each other's hearts. The danger and the force of it all sometimes gave him a fright.

"Eliza, I will keep you," said Adam.

"FINALLY HE SAYS they keep transforming his chamber pot all night long into *a vase of aromatic perfume*."

"Who?" asked Naomi.

"Proust," said Cameron.

"No, I mean who are 'they'?"

"He's still talking about asparagus. As creatures."

"Oh. Animals?" said Naomi.

"Not animals," Cameron said. "Beings. Exquisite beings."

"BESIDES," SAID OLD Nat Morrill to old Leah Cohen, raising his large hand and wanting to put it on her sleeve but letting it drop to the table. "There's no real need for animal meat at all. A single apple gives you as much protein as a side of beef."

"AND GIVE HER your attention," Harry whispered to Adam.

"Eliza, I will give you my attention," Adam echoed.

"Eliza? Harry? Adam? What are you three whispering about down there? Still planning your charades? Can't it wait until after dinner? It's getting a bit impolite, you know."

"No, no, Philippa dear," said Leah. "They're behaving correctly; they're discussing the nature of marriage. . . ."

"Well," broke in William Barlow, "if they figure it out, I hope they'll tell the rest of us."

Everyone laughed politely; Olivia gripped Barnes's arm for a moment.

"Oh, marriage, marriage," Nat Morrill growled. "I never married half the girls I really loved."

"And you, Liz," Harry said in a joking voice, afraid now to whisper, lest he draw attention to himself. "Men are more difficult, you know, than cows. Would you consider growing old?"

"Old?"

"OLDEST OR YOUNGEST? Who goes first, I mean," ten-year-old Harriet whispered to the other children. She fiddled with her buttons. "It better be Eli because he doesn't talk. If anybody asks, we can say he's gone to the bathroom. One of us should go with him; he's too young to go alone."

"I'll go last," said Laurie. "Of course, you don't know if I'll tell on all of you. Or I might stay here and simply eat up all the dessert. But probably I won't."

LARISSA TURNED TO her brother-in-law. "What is it, Cam? You're not eating. You look all strange."

Cameron shook his head unknowingly. Filled with longing, his attention elsewhere, he was unable to do more than put his hand on Issa's shoulder to assure and dismiss her.

"You're sure?" she said.

Cameron nodded.

• • •

"Nathan Morrill, you are dumbfounding me," said Leah. "A side of beef? Less protein than an apple? Are you quite sure? Half a cow?"

"A smallish cow is what I'm speaking about," Nat Morrill insisted. "But I'm not speaking about a calf."

"You were a chef and still you say this?"

"I was and do."

"With him." Harry looked at Adam.

"Oh, grow old with him." Eliza gulped at her wine. "Of course. I would even give him the rest of my wine. . . ."

"Liz, you have to say it better," said Harry softly.

"Adam," Eliza started. Then she froze with a half smile on her face and her hand half cupped around her wineglass. She saw suddenly that if tomorrow's ceremony was a formality simply to please parents and clans, then this secret ritual was the real one. These clandestine utterances were dreadful and important. If she took this one as a lark it would be as meaningless to her as the parental forms that she was casting off. Only if she could say her part correctly, now, would she emerge from this dinner table, her marriage altar, changed. She felt stripped and naked and nightmarishly unprepared to be examined in the language of ritual. She did not know how to receive or contain the spell.

Suddenly alone, Eliza had fallen into the hole at the center of the language of lawyers—the abyss whose presence their protective edifices had evolved to hide—even while pointing at it. In order for this all to work, this secret intimate rite, she would have to construct her soul in a few moments, in the space of a few words. First she would have to recognize that she had no idea what marriage meant. Perhaps no one did—so many did it so poorly. Worse, though, she would have to slip out of being, until she no longer knew what *I* meant, the *I* that was to utter the marriage words. She would have to split apart into atoms and then build herself up again. Eliza sat deathly still, brushed by wings.

Harry willed his sister to remake herself, here, between sentences, in the middle of the dinner party, where the parents did not know that she was marrying during the asparagus course, where even Adam did not know what she was going through, where she herself might not have the words for what she was doing. How could one say in public how one would feel and behave in private over years and decades? The distance was so great; the ritual language only served to obscure the distinction between utterance and observance, the terrifying sacrament of promise.

Eliza sat there, barely touching the bowl of her wineglass.

Harry watched how Nathan Morrill and Leah Cohen were leaning toward each other; his brother Babar and Babar's wife, Issa, sitting far from each other, seemed to be further averted than their distance along the table would account for. He followed them with his eyes, hoping that Eliza would catch the way that *existence* emerged from the language of the body, hoping that she would see this hint that the others were inadvertently sending her, as they swayed toward each other or away.

Eliza leaned toward Adam.

"Liz?" Adam said. "Where have you fled to?"

Harry was shiver-happy with the way the wedding was splicing itself into the dinner table conversation; the way it gave a snaking quality to time, slithery and strong, spiraling in order to move forward or backward, a subjunctive contrary-to-fact sort of time, as well as an upside-downness to it all. Catercorner. Topsy-turvy.

"Lizzie?" Adam said. His fork, with a stalk of asparagus speared on it, hovered in midair, as though he thought maybe one should refrain from eating during these moments.

Eliza shook her head with the slightest movement and lifted a finger, hesitantly, vaguely, to show she needed time.

Harry nodded slightly, to tell her she was right: She couldn't answer them yet or all would be lost. All around her people were engaged in construction with words, lawyers and poets, critics and linguists and journalists, but what was really happening, he willed her to see, was simply the play of their bodies, more eloquent and more truthful. He wondered if she could seize that what *being* meant was how she walked through the rooms of her life in all her daily ordinariness.

What you have to trust, he told her silently, is the continuous history of ritual going all the way back. The extreme age of the wedding ceremony. Descent and derivation.

It was all his fault, Harry thought, if his sister didn't see any of the things he had been trying silently to convey. Why had he not spoken to her about this yesterday, or the day before?

"Adam," Eliza said again. "I will take you and keep you and give you light and dark wine and perhaps children. In spring, after we have planted, I will sit and watch the warm rains with you on the covered porch. In summer and in fall I will walk with you in the gardens. And when the snows of winter come, I will wrap us both in a quilt of starry darkness."

• • •

CELIA LOOKED UP and down the length of the table. The heat of yearnings, conspicuous and latent, shimmered the air. There was her daughter Naomi talking with Eliza's brother Cameron, entangling each other in neon threads. They couldn't be serious! This man had no business with Naomi. His life lay elsewhere. And who knew where Naomi's life lay. And yet, Celia had to admit, her daughter looked happy and playful, almost robust. Then, too, if Naomi were involved with someone here at home, she might not need to fly off on her devastating missions. But Naomi was still raw, so newly healed. What could she handle? Oh Christ, she was forgetting, not only was he a Barlow, he was married. Stop it, Naomi. Back off.

Celia had wished for all her brood to find mates. But oh, why had she not been more careful in her wishes? Pindar was always so prudent in the formulation of his wants, but she just wished haphazardly, and look what had happened: Adam was with someone who might never understand him; Sara had lost her head over a man of the cloth—charming, but the wrong cloth because celibate. Though she wouldn't have wanted her own cloth, either: some old fly-specked rabbi who would feel married half to God, leaving only the other, lesser half of himself for Sara. No, all cloth was undesirable for marriage, she thought.

"OH, HEART," DENNIS whispered. "Last dinner for the two of us? What are you talking about? Are you leaving me?"

"I thought you had decided that it was time for both of us to leave each other," Sara said softly. "Isn't that what you meant by 'We have to talk'? In my experience, that is what it always means."

"Perhaps I have much less experience in these things," he said. "But no, that isn't what I meant at all."

They sat not quite touching, yet the sleeve of his white shirt at times brushed her bare arm. What did they want from each other? What could they give?

CAM WATCHED NAOMI. What was it about beauty that made it hard for him to take enough breath? He wondered if he should sob; that would give him more air. He couldn't stop looking at her. He thought of the smoked glass one was supposed to use to look at the sun during an eclipse. Surely this much beauty must be an evolutionary mistake: To steal the breath of onlookers cannot lead to increase of the human species. Perhaps such beauty didn't have anything to do with humans. Perhaps he was merely standing in the path of something else, caught in the crossfire of the gods as they signal with their sacred mirrors.

LISTENING TO PHILIPPA Barlow, watching her gestures, Pindar saw himself as a sort of still center, like the inner core of the axle of a giant cart, with everything revolving around him, not because of any power or importance of his own but rather because of some inner stillness. This came not from being without desires but from hundreds of tiny yearnings that pulled at him like threads, so many that they seemed to cancel one another out, most or all of them being for the things he loved to stay unchanged. He could not tell if his feeling of stillness was a deep happiness, the exhalation of meaning that the gods had breathed into him, or simply the quiet inhalation at the leading edge of chaos and disruption. Everything was turning around him, and he could feel the whistling roar of it all.

Pindar had to do this alone. He could try to tell Celia, but it was something that was in the doing rather than in the telling; talking about it was just a kind of fuzz, a steam emitted from the elements of the doing. It couldn't be told, but it shouldn't be entirely kept silent, either, because then there would be no tradition, no invitation or permission given to others from knowing that someone had found the path.

Pindar noticed his son, Adam, making a gesture with his fists, rotating one under the other as for a brace drill. Adam had caught Sara's eye, and she was laughingly making the gesture back at him. This was one of the oldest things Pindar remembered about himself, this gesture. His parents had always laughed when he did it as a young child, though he had never figured out why. He was about to ask Leah about it, but she was leaning so far toward Nathan Morrill that it seemed as though they were whispering. She was flirting, his mother, in her nineties, not with the beautiful young Harry but with tremulous Nathan Morrill. After all her proclamations about not wanting to be seated next to someone as ancient as she was, she was leading the old man on. Pindar had so many questions for her all of a sudden. Why had he never asked? He wanted to know about Leah's charm, and about his father: Why had Gabriel left the family? Was it some behavior of Leah's, or some caprice of his own? Leah was both noisy and private; she fended off Pindar's questions before he could formulate them. She had that way of diverting, subverting, certain lines of thought that she was unwilling to play with. They seemed to him now to be the ones that would lead most directly to her core.

"Oh, come . . . come . . . come!" Leah said now to Nathan Morrill, laughing. Pindar tried to think of where he had heard that phrase, that invitation. It felt important, but he couldn't place it. Leah had always had a shockingly engaging quality that Pindar lacked, although it had reemerged in his daughter Naomi, who was now happily settled among the other guests. From this distance he couldn't tell if Naomi's fierce attention to the young Barlow fellow was due to courtship or fury. They both looked serious, advancing, falling.

HARRY LEANED TOWARD Adam and Eliza. "Rings were used for marriages four thousand years ago," he said. "Outward and visible sign of an inward and endless love. Oh, Lord, bless this ring, that he who gives it and she who wears it may abide in peace and delight You." Harry reached across the table, as though wanting the salt, and Adam, checking to see that no one was paying attention, took the ring from him. Harry told him what to do and what to say. Adam draped himself around Eliza. Under the tablecloth he took her hand.

DOWN AT THE other end of the table, seven-year-old Liam quietly slipped out of his seat and walked off into the bushes. The ten-year-old girls, Harriet and Laurie, were the only children left.

HEARING HER GRANDMOTHER repeat the word *come,* Sara thought of her parent's friend Jacob, a sometime minister who lived by the sea, and whose definition of prayer was *Please.*

Thank you. Oh. Entreaty. Gratitude. Awe. Perhaps her grand-mother's invocation was actually a fourth kind of prayer: incantation or call. In any case, it seemed a change of dimension from the others, a demand not pertaining to actions, future or past, but simply to be present, to manifest. *Please. Thank you. Oh. Come.*

PHILIPPA HAD BEEN listening to the faint jazzy music coming from the neighboring party beyond the forest. When the saxophone descended to notes too low for her to hear, she tapped Pindar's sleeve. "Eliza tells us that you are working on a book."

Across the table, William Barlow looked at him expectantly. Pindar tried to think of what he could tell them about cooking in the ancient Near East, but he took fright. "I had a friend," he began. He hoped they would not notice that he was completely avoiding Philippa's question. "She told me once that the only Greek witch she ever knew wrote rhyming couplets to foxes on white papers and tied them to trees with string."

Again Philippa Barlow looked at Pindar; she was sure that the real party was not here with this madman, but in some neighboring elsewhere that she could just hear beyond the trees. At that other, luxurious gathering—the one she was missing—people were elegant and beautiful. They were having a marvelous time. They had ideas that didn't tumble out of their mouths like rocks falling from a cliff. At that party farther up the street, the people made themselves understood; their irony was clear, their joking transparent. She looked at Pindar to see if he was serious. How to respond to his new outburst about couplet-writing witches? She did not know any witches. He had the mouth of a turtle, Pindar Cohen, and rather too much beard, gray and black and white. It looked a bit anatomical, his beard, with his too-red mouth half-hidden. He always seemed to be chewing at something. "Foxes," she said at last. She drank some wine. She was going to need as much as she could swallow. "Your friend, she writes poems to foxes."

"No, no, no. Correction," Pindar laughed, delighted that he had managed to sidetrack her from his book. "My friend knew a witch in Greece, who is no longer living, alas, and that witch was the woman who wrote to foxes. Couplets, she said. I suppose they rhymed."

"But why don't you ask your friend about this witch that she knew?" said William.

"You're right, of course. That is what I should do. But my friend is no longer living, so I can't ask her and she can't tell me about the witch."

"It's a striking image," William said. "A tree hung round with white papers to foxes."

Issa Barlow, on Pindar's right, joined in. "They do that in Japan, you know. Rather a lot."

"Poems to foxes?"

"Perhaps, but I mean they're always tying white paper on strings around trees—it looks as though the trees have necklaces or garter belts. Are you sure your witch friend wasn't Japanese? Their spirit world is full of foxes. They are called *kitsune,* and some are divine and some are mischievous or wicked." Issa smiled and gulped her wine.

"But what would one write to a fox about?" asked Philippa, interrupting the direction her daughter-in-law was going in. Larissa's concentration on matters Japanese, including her new nickname, apparently after some poet, seemed dangerous and was most likely linked to whatever was wrong with her marriage. Barnes was so silent these days, so submerged in unhappiness, that Philippa could not get herself to ask him about it. The most she had been able to do was to try to steer all talk away from mention of things Japanese.

"Oh, Fox," said Issa brightly. "Keep away from my chickens and do not mate with my dog." She looked at Pindar, holding out her empty wineglass. "Actually," she added, "in Japan the foxes often take human form and mate with just about everybody."

Philippa stiffened.

"What *many things* do you actually know, oh, Fox?" said Pindar. "Foxes are full of slyness," he went on. "But I think they have no sense of humor. If I had to write to animals, I'd write to goats. I would write hymns to them, not couplets. I have heard rumors"—he paused, gazing first at Philippa and then at Larissa, and giving a brief nod to William—"that goats discovered coffee. Somewhere in Africa. Do you think this is true?"

Philippa laughed nervously. Issa laughed with her and the two women caught each other's eye. "We shall have to ask my daughter, Eliza," said Philippa, looking for solid ground. "She knows animals. But you were going to tell me about your book."

"Absolutely. Yes." He meant, *Not if I can help it.*

"CHOOSE INCOHERENCE?" STEPHEN Barlow asked.

Celia scanned the table before answering. Naomi was leaning forward to speak to Cameron. Eliza and Adam were up to some sort of monkey business, passing something hidden across the table to Harry. Some of the children had disappeared. "Sometimes incoherence is what can throw light on the matter," she said.

"But how supremely useless," Stephen sputtered. "Frivolous.

You might as well have traffic lights in blue and orange and purple. If you want your troops to capture a hill, or bomb a building, you have to tell them which hill, which street and building. With no ambiguity."

"Ah, but we were not talking of bombing," Celia said, her voice almost aggressively soft. "We were talking of poetry and law." She glanced again at Adam and Eliza. Perhaps they were playing one of their word games. She wondered if she ought to nudge them toward better manners.

"Don't you think that there is something rather, how should I say it—sacred—about clarity?" Stephen coughed and reddened at his own use of the word *sacred,* underlining and disowning his earnestness. It was odd, he thought, the sort of things this conversation brought out in him. He wondered if Pippa was having as strange a time as he was. He found himself asking, "Doesn't the universal foggy-mindedness bother you?"

Celia winced at the word *universal.*

Stephen Barlow went on. "Legal language strips away the mess, the individual particularities; it reduces everything—people, relationships, actions—to their fundamental structures. Then we can actually see them, like pieces on a game board; we can work with them."

"But those messes you've jettisoned!" Celia said. "Those tangles of particularity—that is where our humanity resides. When you look at humans as game pieces, aren't you throwing out truth along with the confusion?"

"But we are trying to clarify," he said. "While the poets . . ." He seemed helpless to finish his own sentence, to speak to this being who was so other. He waved his hand loosely.

"In the domain of the rational," Celia began, "language

works in a linear manner. It has to, so that things can be written down, one well-defined word at a time, like beads on a string. In the law you do this by stripping things down to fundamentals, to ciphers.

"Think of poems as trying to get beyond the gates of the rational to a place where everything is happening at once, where the human messes and particulars are tangled with the undergrowth of things in ways that cannot easily be described. In the language of this domain each word seems alive with possible meanings, overtones and resonances, leading to wild evocations, ambiguities, and even contradictions. Things no longer work solely in a linear order. It's like making an embroidery— the words and meanings are all interwoven. What seems like incoherence on one level may be expressing subtleties and truths on another."

Stephen Barlow was silent for a while. "I don't know what you mean," he said. "I don't know how to think like that."

A cardinal landed high in the old pine at the edge of the garden, where it proceeded to give a series of calls. Celia waited until they could hear its mate respond in the distance. She smiled. "It's like taking a walk," she said gently. "In a forest. An ordinary forest."

"But this is like a bad dream," Leah Cohen burst out. "It's such a perverse doctrine. Will your friend allow curry powder on her raw foods?"

"Not allowed, my dear," said Nat Morrill. "Curry powder is already a mixture, thus impure. In any case, she does not allow one to sprinkle something on top of something else."

"This is worse than kashruth," Leah said. "What about sushi?"

"Not allowed. It's raw, but still, it's a combination, because of the rice, the seaweed."

"Sashimi?"

"Fine. But no joining, no marriage of the fish with soy sauce or pickled ginger, no green shiso leaf."

No one could see Adam slipping a ring onto Eliza's finger. Only Eliza could hear him consecrate himself. Harry blessed the other ring and gave it to Eliza. "Say what Adam did, and do the same."

The pale-skinned girl slipped up to the table and sat quietly in the seat recently vacated by seven-year-old Liam. She nodded to Harriet and Laurie. The three ten-year-old girls eyed one another.

"Hi," said Laurie. "You must be from the other side?"

"I am Leila. Sometimes I don't know where I'm from. I'm supposed to be at the party with all the music, but I got turned around in the woods when I tried to take a walk. I like your party better. I saw you all stealing away and I thought it would be good if I filled in here for a while. So the grown-ups don't notice anything."

Even gawky Harriet, with her untucked blouse and tangled hair, looked robust beside the new girl. "Will you come to the pond with us?"

"Yes, if you let me catch my breath. I've been racing about."

· · ·

"YOUR BOOK," PHILIPPA persisted.

"Well," Pindar said. "I've been wondering if perhaps our greatest appetite"—he paused here, then finished—"is really for sleep."

Philippa drew back, as though he had said he wanted to bed her.

Pindar tugged at his beard, exposing more of the redness of his lips. "We long for it. We can't give it up. Even the Babylonians knew this, three thousand years ago. For them it was part of our humanity, a sign of our mortality. To gain life everlasting, the greatest Babylonian hero, a man-god, is given the test of staying awake for six days and seven nights. Of course he fails miserably, dozing off the minute he hunkers down on his haunches."

"So your book is about sleep," William Barlow said.

"Not exactly," Pindar stalled. "Let me just dash in to the house for a moment and get us some more wine. Then I'll tell you."

"WHERE DO YOU put a sky like that?" Leah said to Nathan, pointing to the first streaks of rose gold in a pair of high clouds. "Where do you . . . well, in what compartment?"

"Do you mean . . ."

"Yes. I mean, shouldn't it be stowed somewhere, so it isn't lost? How does it affect, otherwise?"

"Affect me? You? The world?"

"Not the world. You. Me. How do you put it somewhere so

that its effect on you is something? How do you file it? How do you store it?"

"Store," he echoed. He had the sudden image of her taking a sunset and shaking it out like some infinite orange and red and purple blanket, shaking and folding and leveling it, folding it small enough so she could slide it into a cupboard, an armoire. Smelling of, no, he couldn't yet put a name to the smell. The nature of that wardrobe confused him. How large would it have to be to hold the folded evening sky? It wasn't tidiness one was after. By putting it somewhere, she must have meant deciding how watching the heralded sunset, even having been watched by the sunset, pressed on him, changed him, until it became part of who he was.

"YOU'LL NEVER CATCH me getting married," said ten-year-old Laurie, moving the food around on her plate but not eating it. She leaned forward, shook her ash-blond hair into her face, then out of it.

"How come?" asked Harriet.

"Look at my parents: My mom is an angel. My dad leaves her every month to go to his law firm's office in Paris. There he eats butter like a pig, smokes French cigarettes, and fornicates his mistress. He and his mistress have a disgustingly perfect son named Guillaume, who is only a few months younger than me, who speaks disgustingly perfect French, disgustingly perfect English. . . ."

"Who told you this?" asked Harriet.

"No one," said Laurie. "No one will ever tell you. You have to hunt for all the important things yourself. All grown-ups have terrible secrets. You must look in their pockets before your mother or the cleaning lady gets there. My dad never talks about these French people. I heard him talking French on the phone one day when he thought no one was home, and I listened. First there was this lady, and then there was this boy on the other end, calling him Papa. I listen in when I can. Perhaps I'll marry Guillaume when I grow up, just to show them."

"But you just said you'll never marry," said Harriet, who could always spot disorders of logic.

". . . CONSECRATE YOU TO me," Eliza whispered to Adam.

"As I started to say in the attic," Harry said, "for Christians, marriage is in the spoken promises; for Jews, it's with the exchange of rings; for Muslims, in the signing of the contract. . . ."

"But what if we both dropped dead after the promises and before the rings?" Eliza asked. "Would I be married and Adam not?"

"Hush," whispered Harry. He looked around, up and down the table. No one was paying attention to them. "Holding hands shows that a binding contract is occurring. Before God, and Leah, who is your only knowing witness, and all these others, who have no clue, and all the bats of evening, you have pledged yourselves. Husband and wife, may God take pleasure in you both. When you get up from this table, you are not as you came to it. Although the families don't yet know it, your place among them has changed."

A PAIR OF bats appear, as though called, first one, then perhaps its mate, darting, lifting.

• • •

"You are completely wrong," said Dennis. "We are not leaving each other. I am ashamed for having let you or led you to think that. You should know me better than that. I said we had to talk—face-to-face—because I want to convince you to come to Africa with me this summer."

Sara could feel her face redden at her mistake. She could not look in his direction and pretended not to hear him. She waved to her grandmother and lifted her wineglass, the two women toasting each other across the table and through the generations. When Sara put her glass down, she spilled the wine that remained. She blotted it with her napkin as though blotting out her whole conversation with Dennis, the daylong misunderstanding, and the new and alarming proposition of following him to Africa. She hadn't even had time to savor her relief before this new question took over the landscape. She reeled at the quickness of happenings, then left the table again to go into the house and get a napkin.

Dennis touched her arm as she left. "Don't be long," he said.

"Sorry?" Cameron Barlow said to Naomi Cohen. "I missed that. What new pleasure? What did you say?"

"Let me explain," Naomi said. "I was driving to the sea"—she leaned across the table toward him—"to meet a group of friends for dinner at a small restaurant. I was happy. And suddenly as I passed the cornfield before the plant nursery, I realized that I was walking or running on top of the corn. I could feel the tassels under my feet, slightly raspy and tickling the soles of my feet. And that's how I knew I really was then—for those moments—on top of the corn, above the corn, because I could *feel* it, rather than in the car, which I couldn't feel. There was an intensity of being, out there on top of the corn, which I couldn't deny or explain. The memory stayed in my feet and calves all through dinner."

"Do you do this often, this dancing on corn?" Cam asked.

"Never."

"Would you stop it if I asked you?"

"Why would you do that? I am just learning how."

Cam could not answer. It did not seem safe to have Naomi hovering above the grain. That was not where he wanted her, unless he could join her there, and he knew that was unlikely.

"If I were to die," Naomi blurted, "the entire burden of our friendship with each other would fall onto you."

"Die? Are you planning to?"

"Not at all." She gave a clear laugh. "I'm so sorry." She laughed again, inviting him. "I have no idea where that thought came from. Besides, we've known each other a matter of hours. Less."

"Now that I am so old," Leah was explaining to Nathan, "I live in Cambridge. I like to be where ideas make the air all fizzy. Otherwise I would stagnate like a swamp and my days would seep away. You have to be where other people are constantly learning when you yourself are approaching the age of forgetting. I am not at that age yet, but my friends are. I show up for lunch and they have cooked nothing: They have forgotten they invited me, although it was that same morning they had telephoned. I live alone. My friend Miriam used to come for long visits—we were together in Paris when we were very young; we wrote, she danced, and both of us generally misbehaved. She is dead now. They do begin to flutter off, one's friends. At first, I thought of it as a competition, staying alive. But then you find that you have won but you are alone. They are dead, mostly, my friends. I think you learn to watch them go."

"I don't."

"Your friends don't die?"

"No, no. They do," said Nathan Morrill. "But I don't learn. I seem to carry them around with me, their loss, I mean, and it all just gets heavier and heavier. When did your friend die?"

"Miriam? It must have been a decade ago. Oh, Lord. I left Paris in '36, when I was the same age. As the century, I mean. I didn't go home to my parents in Britain, as we had been at odds since . . . forever. I was such an embarrassment to them that they finally sent me to Paris. I loved all the wrong people and refused to marry any of the right ones. They kept wanting me to consort with those little snorty pigs. I suppose I mean *prigs,* but they all had wretched snaggleteeth and flat little piggy noses. When I finally fled France I came to the States, here to Boston; I was already with Gabriel, Pindar's father. It was he who realized that it was unsafe to stay in France. Bless the man. His timing was occasionally perfect."

CELIA WATCHED THE ancient bodies of Pindar's mother and Philippa's father as they swayed toward each other. Nathan Morrill waved his ancient hands like flippers. Clearly he wanted to put one of these appendages on Leah's hands, but something was not allowing it. Celia was pleased by this flirtation. Leah was old enough to do what she wanted. And that one could still find reasons to cavort at ninety-one, well!

• • •

BARNES BARLOW SCANNED the dinner table. *I could probably leave now,* he said to himself. *I could be at home reading a detective novel, watching an old movie, having thoughts.* And he began to count the thoughts he might have but they all cycled back to what he was going to do with his life, now that he had quit his job and his marriage was about to quit him. Government would be the natural direction, but he was weary of doing the expected thing. Besides, that was just another bunch of crooks. Finance did not attract him at all, and he was not at all gifted in the pecuniary direction. But he knew that if he limited himself to where his gifts lay, it was hopeless. How could he talk to anyone at this party when he didn't know where he was headed? Best to be quiet. He had spent his whole life yelling.

LEAH, HAVING WITNESSED the soft-spoken elopement between her poet grandson and his fair-haired girl who could speak to cows, listened now to the call of a bird, high in the dark pine tree behind the garden. The repeated trill was answered by its mate, farther off, and then another, even more distant, reminding her of a time in her youth when she had spent the night in the Jardin du Luxembourg in Paris, waiting for her lover. As night was falling, the police walked through the gardens, blowing their whistles and telling the few people still sitting on their metal chairs that it was closing time. Young Leah had hidden in the bushes until they passed, and there she stayed, eating oranges, until well past midnight, the hour when her lover had promised to appear. When at last he rescued her from her passionate waiting, he was wearing the uniform of a gendarme. They went off to his rooftop apartment. And later, it seemed like days later, when they had inhabited each other until no one else existed, they went out into the streets of a bemused Paris, strolling under the purple sky to a restaurant, where they ate oysters, then a saffron-flavored ice in a cage of spun sugar whose strands they broke with silver spoons. Where was he now, she wondered, that being of darkness? It had been brief, their affair, and she had ended it long before she met Gabriel.

"Listen," Leah said to Nathan Morrill, waking him from sleep. "Hear the night bird, calling out to the distance? Stay awake for a bit and I will tell you of the whistles of evening in Paris, when I was very young."

"AFRICA," DENNIS SAID softly when Sara returned. "I want you to come with me."

"God, it's hot tonight and it's only the first of June," Sara replied. "Don't you want some more wine? Would you like ice? Look at my grandmother. She's clearly attracted to Eliza's grandfather, don't you think? She had threatened my parents that she would bite if they seated her near anyone as old as she is, but now look. She's falling into his arms. Aren't they old for that?"

"Africa," Dennis repeated. "The Gambia. I know I can't really ask this of you, but it would be so glorious to have you there with me. There's just enough time for you to get your shots—a little over three weeks until we leave."

"Did you know that my brother and Eliza tried to elope earlier?"

"What are you talking about?"

"While people were arriving and having drinks," Sara continued. "You were out in the garden, talking to my mother, I think, but we were all up in the attic. Adam asked Grandma Leah and me to be witnesses, but then Philippa Barlow was snooping around and she ferreted us out and scolded us and told us we had to come downstairs. A bit later we all tried to resume the ceremony up at the pond, but then all the little kids were sent to bring us back and we couldn't continue."

"Why are you doing this, my love?" Dennis asked.

FOR THE SECOND time during the dinner party Pindar found himself escaping the table and going into the sanctuary of his house. This need to get away from the gathering was so strong in him that it was like a twitch he couldn't control. Of course he felt guilty about leaving, but he had been behaving rather well, and who was to know that he wasn't simply answering a call of nature? Celia had left the table moments earlier and maybe he could find her. Perhaps they could run away together. They could go to the sea. Glancing into the kitchen he saw Chhaya, who was whipping up a white froth in an immense bowl. Borsuk leaned over, watching her. Not wanting to disturb them Pindar went upstairs without speaking. A small while was all he needed, a moment of darkness.

The bedroom door was locked.

"Who's there?"

"It's me."

"Who?"

"Me," Pindar repeated, louder.

Celia opened the door. "You didn't sound like yourself. Were you whispering?" Celia went back to the mirror and stood there combing her hair. Pindar crept up behind her and looked over her shoulder into the glass, smiling at her. Finally she turned to him.

"Pindar?"

"Mmmn?"

"What are you doing?"

"Mmmn."

"We shouldn't even be here."

"No one will notice."

"Madman. Barlows in the garden."

"They can wait."

When elephants who have been forcefully separated for decades are finally reunited, they will wander through savanna or jungle, caressing each other by entwining their trunks and then walking their bodies back and forth along each other, as though their entire skin had an exquisite sensitivity—as though the whole body were a hand, but more sensitive than our hands are, a hand combining all the senses—and they walk back and forth as though bathing in each other, as though for them touch defines both presence and essence, *being there* and *being*. A sudden definition of self as part of a joining.

From the distant woods, the jazz trumpets and snare drum were still playing dance tunes, sexy and old-fashioned—while from the garden down below came laughter and the clinking of silverware against glass. Someone, it must have been Leah, was toasting: To youth, she said. To love. One of the Barlow men exclaimed about the bat flying overhead. A sliver of late sunlight seeped into the bedroom window and glowed in a trapezoid on the floor. A bird called. Gripped by the panic of love, Pindar groaned.

NAT MORRILL GRABBED the bouquet from the brass vase in front of him with his clawed hands. He held it in his lap, caressing the blue, yellow, and white blossoms as though they were small chicks. He brought his fingers to his nose and sniffed, smiled. He raised the bouquet, shook it a few times, and held it to his ear, to listen.

"What are they telling you, those flowers?" asked Leah.

"Oh dear," he said, as though waking up. "You've caught me listening to flowers as though they were whelks. Perhaps I can hear the forest or the meadow. Well, who knows? Perhaps I am joking."

Leah leaned toward him. "Perhaps you are," she said, perching her hand on his shoulder.

"But will you come visit me?" he asked, trying now to keep any sound of pleading out of his voice. "Will you let me come and see you? Will your companion allow it?"

"My companion? If you mean Miriam, she has been dead these dozen years."

"I forgot. Yes. But may I visit?"

"Of course I will let you visit. We will discuss food. And how to remember."

"Remembering, yes. Food. And love?"

"BABAR." OLIVIA, HIS brother William's wife, put her hand on his. "Babar, where are you? You haven't said a word all evening."

Despite his profession as a prosecuting lawyer, Barnes had always seemed to Olivia to be the gentlest of all her Barlow in-laws. She felt that she and Barnes were unusually linked although they had never done anything to deserve this feeling.

Barnes twitched, then relaxed. Olivia was one of his favorites, inside the family, or outside. "Libby, I know," he said. "I'm sorry. I am an awful dinner partner," he whispered. He hoped she would think he had laryngitis. Perhaps he did. The larynx of the soul.

"Don't be silly," Olivia said. "I'd rather sit beside you than anybody here." Barnes had always seemed to her to have all his brother William's brightness with none of his pomposity or entitledness. She reached for the Pinot Grigio in front of her and poured some into his glass. "What is it, then? Is it very bad?"

"Oh, Lib, it is."

"I thought so. I've watched it come over you."

Barnes sat back, startled. "Does it show?" Worry darkened him.

"It has come to cover you like a blanket: desire—"

"Oh, it's not desire," Barnes interrupted, disappointed that she hadn't understood and relieved that his ailment didn't show. He kept a hand in front of his mouth as he spoke.

"You didn't let me finish. What shows—what I see, at least—is *desire not to talk*. Not to say a word."

"Can you see? Can other people see it?"

"Not unless they already know. This is something that I happen to understand." Olivia knew a few forms of verbal reluctance, from her own refusing to mention William's mistress in Paris to the selective muteness of their three-year-old son, Eli. She paused and looked around at all the guests talking and listening. Directly across from her, Nathan Morrill had placed his large flat hand on old Leah Cohen's purple sleeve. Beside Leah, William's youngest brother, Harry, was leaning toward Eliza and Adam and whispering as though blessing them. The children had gone somewhere, had crept away, taking her silent little Eli with them. His sister, Laurie, would watch him; she was good at that, even though she could be ingeniously bossy. Poor little Eli, who had been pronounced fine by the pediatrician; the

ear, nose, and throat man; the audiologists; and the speech therapists. Well, they didn't say he was fine but said he would ben-
efit from lessons. "Give him time," they all said. "Be patient."
She did give Eli time, and often she even felt that she knew what
was going on inside his three-year-old mind. But his silence
tugged at her heart and pulled at her throat, especially in the
evenings when she put him to bed and read him a story. One
night, when she sang him a song after reading, she thought she
could hear him humming under his breath, and so each night
she repeated her singing, hoping that one evening he would follow her and slip, without noticing, into song. Speaking might
follow, she thought. Real words. Always Olivia was calm and
persistent and patient. There were times when she wasn't sure
she could bear it. She kept her focus on Eli to divert her thoughts
from William and what he was doing in Paris.

Olivia turned back to Barnes. "What about written things?
Can you read, or is it there, too?"

"I can read. As long as I don't vocalize."

"What does Issa say?"

"The more she talks, the less I feel like saying. Then she prac-
tices her Japanese tapes. We're separating."

"Oh, Babar. I'm so sorry. I wondered if you were."

CELIA AND PINDAR came out of the house each carrying a
couple of bottles of wine.

"YOU'VE GOT TO stop this, my love," Dennis said.

Sara shook her head. "Look," she said. "I don't even know
if it's called Gambia or the Gambia."

"It changes officially from time to time. Everyone has a different opinion about what to call it, and that opinion, too, can change from one day to the next. As far as I can tell, right now it's 'the.' But that is not what we're talking about."

"Well, it is, sort of. How can I say if I will come to a place with you when I don't even know its name?"

"Unnamed territory is often the most interesting."

CAM WAS STILL watching Naomi. It wasn't that she was classically beautiful, but she was delicate in a way that made him want to be with her, listen to her, take care of her. Her posture, the way she cocked her head, stretched her slender arms when she pointed to things in the garden, the way she laughed, these were captivating him, as well as her odd combination of seeming mischievous and earnest and knowing. There was something extremely young and very old about her. She made him feel suddenly awake, alert, full of jitters. He looked down the table at his wife and children to try to ground himself, but Amy was facing away from him, Liam had left the table, and Emily was looking at a bug on her finger. Cam turned back to Naomi.

PINDAR SAW THAT Celia was looking at him. She tapped her forefinger on the side of her water glass. Was she telling him to drink water instead of wine? He glanced around the table. The guests turned toward him, suddenly quiet, all the grown-ups, the children having gone off somewhere. Celia gestured by tapping her glass again. Ah, the toast. He was supposed to toast the young couple. She had tried to remind him earlier to think about it, but his mind had been on other things. Now all those faces were gazing at him, expectant, beaming. He hadn't prepared a word. He would have to think it out during this smiling attentive silence in the course of clinking his knife against his glass. He loved giving talks, but he needed a breath or two. He leaned forward in his seat, bracing his hands on his thighs. He felt relaxed and sweet; perhaps it was the wine.

The fragrance of the pine trees at the edge of the garden made him want his pipe, but his mission at the moment was with words of blessing and approval. His complete attention should be on Adam and Eliza, without even a filament of digression. As he got to his feet, his back, which usually gnawed at him, was purring. He looked at the forest; he looked at the gathered company. "Earth, air, fire, and water," he began. "The ancient Greek philosopher Empedocles says that these four elements are the roots of everything."

Here was the garden he inherited from Leah. Celia, who mostly tended it, called it her sculpture in four dimensions, the fourth being time. Perhaps all sculpture changed over time, with decay and dissolution setting in, rust and chipping and breakage. But marble or bronze evolved so slowly, and their changes were unintended, while the garden was always in visible flux, each morning a new unfolding. Celia always said that the flower beds were a progression of looping actions: each plant opening, blooming, fading, setting seed, drooping, falling; and each seed rooting, sprouting, budding, blooming. And the seasons, the moons and days, the pendulum of darkness and light, the beat of the cardinal's song. Was the earth, then, our real timepiece? Stop, Pindar. Pay attention.

"But Empedocles also said that our spirits have successive lives, born sometimes as the fair-tressed laurel trees, sometimes as lions who live in the golden grass. . . ."

A shifting of the light through the trees made Pindar notice the Queen Anne's lace in its brass vase. Constellations of tiny white stars swirled in a galactic umbrella the size of his hand—who was above? Who below? Beside their lacy flaring explosive symmetry, the black-eyed Susans gazed at him with their fierce yellow. Wide-open, with none of the hidden turns and caverns of the lilies whose trumpets would be deep enough to incubate in, or at least hide one's thoughts in, though their scent would be too strong for the dinner table. Damn it. Stop this. He could see that his silence had made everyone uncomfortable.

"Finally, Empedocles says, after being lions and laurel trees we appear as prophets, poets, doctors, and lawgivers." Pindar pointed in turn to Harry, Adam, Eliza, and then with a broad sweep of his arm to the rest of the Barlow family. "This is the last stage before our spirits rise to the ranks of the immortals, where beyond human weakness and sorrow we live with the gods and join them at their feasts."

Pindar knew he was not supposed to be lost in flowers right now. Nor in Babylon. Though he could see slipping in from the edge of his mind that what he was looking for was somehow connected with flowers, and that redefining the nature of time in terms of gardens meant that he could perform his search, here, in the midst of this toast to his son and future daughter-in-law. Even with the hanging gardens of Babylon now swinging into his mind—terraced and swinging low as that chariot of the ancient poet Parmenides, wheeling so fast that a cosmic whistling roar sounded from its axles as it took him to the underworld—no. No. Back to Empedocles, who had also gone down to the underworld; Empedocles, like Parmenides, was both a poet and lawgiver. Poetry and law. Whew. He was home now. Pindar smiled out at the company and raised his glass.

"So prophets, poets, doctors, and lawgivers are next to the gods. Empedocles embodied all four of these callings in one person. And we, Barlows and Cohens, by joining ourselves with the marriage of Eliza and Adam, will combine these vocations in one family. In the tradition Empedocles came from, the poet would sometimes go and lie down in an underground cave for several days, going into a trance while a priest kept watch against bears. And from this trance, the poet would awaken with a prophetic vision, often having to do with new laws. . . ."

Not quite sure how to bring this all to a close, Pindar braced his hands on the table and shifted his weight from one leg to the other, releasing a stiffness that had crept into his back. Setting his left foot down, he happened to place it too close to one of the clay pots holding a citronella candle. A thin tongue of flame licked up his pant leg. There came a smell of burning cloth.

"Good God." Philippa Barlow leaped up. "The man is on fire. Somebody do something." She hoped no one noticed she had taken her sandals off.

Larissa Barlow threw the water from her untouched glass on Pindar's leg. She then reached for the pitcher and doused him with more water, just to make sure.

"Thank you, my dear," Pindar said to Issa. "I'm very grateful." He dabbed at his charred pant leg with his napkin, happy to feel that there was no burn. "No harm done," he announced with a smile. "I didn't mean to go into a whole lecture here," he continued. "I just wanted to say what an old and venerable tradition it is to join together the ideas and the practitioners of poetry, law, healing, and prophecy—perhaps we should add firefighters as well. Let us drink to Eliza and Adam."

• • •

SARA LOOKED STRAIGHT at Dennis. "What on earth would I do in Africa? Here I have my scorpion folklore project, but there nothing at all." She added, "Except you."

"Here you have only libraries. There you would have the world. There are so many scorpions there that the Gambian national soccer team is named after them. Also, I have some strange archives there, part of a project I've been researching on my own for years, having to do with magic and medicine up-river. I haven't published any of it yet and I have records that may be crucial for you. But it's not just my archives, for they, too, are just texts—even if they are unique. It's the people you should see, the people in the compound where I live. If you are doing folklore, you should see my friends there and how they think of and interact with your dangerous little beast."

Sara was silent. She pictured scorpions playing soccer. She was trying to avoid the real problem of what he was proposing. "But think of how awkward it would be," she finally burst out. "All that skulking about, traveling with a priest. Where would I live? When would I get to see you?"

"You would live with me in my house in the compound. That is how it's done upriver. It wouldn't be awkward at all. It's not like here. We would live openly. It is a small house, but beautifully adequate. There is a desk for you, a place to work. Please say that you will consider it."

"I will consider it," she said. But she was still puzzled. "Three weeks . . . If you really wanted me to come, why did you wait until so late to ask me?"

"Pure selfishness," he said. "I wanted to leave it as late as I could so that I could keep my hopes up as long as possible. As long as I didn't ask you, you couldn't refuse."

"And after?" Sara said. "What happens to us when we get back?"

"We will face that territory when we get to it. I think we would hate ourselves if we didn't try this."

LEAH LISTENED TO all the sounds around her, the distant laughter of the children at the pond, the needles of the pine trees brushing against one another in the grove behind the garden, and the breathing of the dinner party itself: the clamor of forks on plates, the muttering of the chairs, the creaking of the old tables where they rubbed up against each other under the white cloth, the flickering of the candles, the rising of the bubbles in the mineral water, the shifting of lettuce leaves in the wooden salad bowl. And she noticed that the noise that had always been in her head, the sound like an alarm with no name, had stopped suddenly, and though she had never been conscious of it while it was there—it had been with her all her adult life and maybe longer—now its absence made her notice it and allowed her to name it to herself. And she knew it was some sort of sign, this new inner stillness, and though she was not a worrier by nature she wondered if the previously unnoticed noises of the evening were what she should be listening to, or if she had been granted this silence in order to be able to hear some new and different thing. Now, for the moment, her head was clear and without echo.

PART FIVE

Meanwhile
the
Children

Off in the woods, away from the garden party, where their parents and grandparents were sitting at the long table eating asparagus and drinking wine, the children's time became their own. The sky was still bright, as though it would never darken, but at the pond twilight spread itself between the trees as though it had no beginning and no end.

Seven-year-old Liam was the first of the children to walk into the pond. He had taken off his shorts and sandals, and now he stood there in his underpants, in water up to his waist, his feet rejoicing in the sweet muck at the bottom. The evening air was warm and the water was warm and smelled of leaves and mud and fish, and he liked, too, the occasional flick of a fish against his bare legs. He was glad that they had all had the sense to slide away from the grown-ups, although he liked his aunt Lizzie and the man she was marrying. It was clear, though, that the asparagus would go on forever. He had lost hope of any other food.

Liam's three-year-old cousin, Eli, sat on the grass at the edge of the water, working at his shoes, wondering about his shoelaces and the nature of the knots they got into without any help from him. Sometimes the laces refused to unwind, even when they didn't seem locked up, and other times what seemed to be knots were really loops that came apart with only a pull; there was no telling. There was also no asking, as Eli had chosen to live without speaking when other people were present. At first he had wondered whether it was worth the trips to doctors and clinics and speech therapists, but those had tapered off now with only weekly trips to the speech lady. He sometimes gave her a grunt or a squeak, sensing that these would keep her interested, but nothing more, and he did this only when she had her back to him, so she could never be quite sure.

Liam's sister, Emily, hung her yellow dress over the back of the garden bench and placed her shoes and socks beside it. She pranced about in underpants, her eight-year-old body tight and long as a string bean. She cartwheeled on the grass, then knelt to help her cousin Eli with his laces, telling him to take his clothes off and put them far from the water in case there was splashing. She didn't talk to him as though he were deaf or stupid, and he was grateful to her. The pond was shallow and clear at the edges; farther out its surface was ribbed with reflections of the apple green of dusk. Emily stepped in and walked to deeper water, chanting, "It's not cold, it's not cold." She scanned for dragonflies but found only a water skeeter and followed it instead.

Liberated from shoes and trousers and button-down shirt, little Eli slid into the pond and began a slow paddling around the edge, hands touching the soft old leaves on the bottom. Emily waded over to him to make sure he didn't go too deep.

The older girls, the ten-year-olds, had remained at the table in the garden for a while, but soon they, too, slipped away and went running through the woods, their bright-colored dresses glinting through the trees. Laurie had not stayed behind to eat all their desserts as she had threatened, and now, silent and quick, feeling the absurd freedom of having left the grown-ups, she felt like laughing aloud but kept herself from sound. Beside her, dark-haired Harriet ran gracefully as soon as she was out of sight of her parents.

At the pond the trio of ten-year-olds began to strip as though for a well-known ritual: shoes off, socks in the shoes. Laurie stalled a bit, stricken now by the problem of getting undressed in front of the others. She peered over at her little brother, Eli, to make sure he was safe, and then looked down at the grass as she pulled off her dress and hugged her unbudded breasts as she skittered off toward the water.

Harriet, having cast off her skirt and blouse, no longer seemed disordered or askew; her brown frizzy hair fanned out around her face, framing her loveliness, crowning her. In semi-nakedness she walked along the verge like a young queen. Feeling the warm evening breeze on her body, she smiled. And noticing how tentative and body-shy her quick-tongued cousin Laurie was, she gloated.

Leila, the pale girl who had accompanied them, was the only one who removed all her clothes. Her white form moved through the shadows. Harriet wanted to say something to her, ask her something crucial, but Liam was asking Emily, "What shall we make for dinner? Should it be firefly soup or are we really going to catch fish?"

"It's too early in the year for fireflies, even though it's so hot," Emily said. "Let's see what kind of fish are here and how they behave."

Liam put his arms out from his sides, hands lightly touching the water's surface as though to quiet it.

"Aren't they all carp?" asked Laurie, crouching down in the pond so as to stay submerged up to her chin. No one must see her breasts, even though she didn't have them yet. She knew they wouldn't grow if they were looked at.

"Maybe. But there are many carps. Besides . . ." Liam paused, not wanting to frighten the girls.

"Besides?" said Harriet. She stepped in, wondering why she didn't live in the water, it was so welcoming and warm.

Liam, lover of fish, kept silent.

"What he means," began Leila, "what he means is that carp can get to be dreadfully ancient."

"A hundred years?" asked Emily.

"More," said the pale girl. "If you like."

"Well," said Laurie. "Do we want to catch a young one or an old one?" She tried to sound matter-of-fact, but the notion of ancient fish spooked her. She stood up now, arms across her chest. "You know," she said. "Right there"—she gestured—"no, over to the left a bit. That's it. The center. That's where the water goes all the way down. That must be where the really old ones come from."

They all looked where she pointed. Although the pond had seemed clear before they all entered the water, now it was murky. They shivered. Harriet at ten was wise enough to know that her cousin was up to something, Laurie usually was, but Harriet did not quite know what, and disarmed by the bald-faced lie—if it was one—she kept silent, taken by the moment. Emily, two years younger, giggled from seriousness and fright.

"Down to China?" Liam croaked. His older cousin Laurie had always been able to bind him with fears.

"At least," Laurie said gravely.

"But it can't be farther than China," Harriet said, her innate sensibleness coming to the surface. "Then it would be out the other side."

"Yes," said Laurie.

"And into the sky?" asked Liam.

"Exactly," said Laurie. "A sort of geyser."

Liam thought he knew better, but he wasn't sure. He knew

quite a bit about fish, and rather less about fluids and geometries at the core of the earth.

They all gazed into the water, wanting to believe that the bottom, though not evident, was close.

Laurie held up one finger. "You know," she began. She was desperate to back off as she knew that she couldn't sustain this mischievous story. "It could have been a different pond. I saw the description in a book, but I didn't pay enough attention. Besides, I think it's rather small, a few inches or so—maybe even the size of a quarter—that forms the really deep part of the exact center. It's easy to miss."

The others didn't know whether to be relieved or not.

"So which kind of carp do we want, anyway?" asked Laurie. "Old or young?" She had been caught off guard by what Liam and the pale girl had said about ancient fish, and wondered if fish could live to be a hundred, and what one ought to do with really old ones. Perhaps her cousins, too, were shaky on their facts.

"Oh, it's hardly a matter of what *we* want," said the pale girl, Leila.

"Yes," said Liam. "It's what the fish are willing to let us do."

Little Eli, the silent one, had been navigating the margins, but now he turned toward them, listening. He wasn't sure why hundred-year-old fish were important, but the conversation made his skin prickle.

Laurie said now, scaring herself, "Old fish with a long white beard, swimming around and watching us and whisking our legs with his old white hair." She stopped, overcome with shivers. Eli reached his small hands out into the water to see if he could touch such a whiskered fish, then drew his arms back close to his body.

White-skinned Leila, standing on the edge, still had not entered the water. She ran back to the bench and fumbled in her clothes, looking for something in her pockets. It was the candle and matches that she had brought from the party where she was supposed to be, the one with all the music. She had told her parents she was going exploring in the woods, and they had seemed happy that she had found something to do. She hadn't quite told them that she was going off alone, but they had been dancing to the band and hadn't asked. She lit the wick and made a puddle of wax on a rock by the edge of the pond, then held the candle upright in it until the wax had hardened.

"Is that for the fish or for us?" Liam asked.

"Look." Leila pointed. A curved shape swam under the surface toward the light she had just made.

Liam threw himself onto the fish in a scuffle of kicking and splashes. He held on as it dragged him away from the banks and down, and he could feel the smooth skin of the body and the thin spines of the fins and the pulsing of the muscles. Then his foot got tangled in some weeds and their tug was enough to make him lose his grip. He surfaced to breathe, then dived under again, looking for the fish, reaching his hands in all directions, but the water was too cloudy to see anything and he felt his lungs would burst. Snorting and coughing he emerged, face and shoulders smeared with mud. "It was immense," he said. "I didn't realize . . ." He could not continue. He took deep breaths, still heaving. Then, calmer, "I think I lost my watch."

"Realize what?" said Laurie, her teeth chattering.

"That this pond would be that old. Or the fish in it so huge. I mean, it was really, really . . . it was as big as Eli."

Hearing this, Eli stood up in the shallows, proud of the comparison. He put his small hand to his chest.

"Yes," said Liam, panting for breath. "Your size, Eli." He turned to the others. "The thing is, he wasn't afraid of me. He didn't mind that I was holding him. But he didn't want to be caught, either. It felt like he just wanted me to notice." Liam stood there while his breath caught up with him.

"Maybe he was just playing with you?" Laurie asked. "But then why did he take your watch?"

"He didn't take it," Liam answered quickly. "It just got lost. It lost itself."

"The sensible thing to do," said Harriet, "would be for us to walk around and see if we can feel your watch with our feet."

They slurred their feet through the feathery ooze, keeping near the grassy edge. After a while Laurie said, "You know, we could try the losing-finding trick—my mother did it once with her contact lenses. She let the second one fall on purpose to see if it would lead her to the first one. It's just a matter of repeating the conditions and paying attention."

"But did it work?" asked Harriet.

"I don't think so," Laurie replied. "I don't remember."

"But we'd need another huge fish," Liam said.

"I think I'd rather not throw my watch," said Harriet.

"Me neither," said Emily. "But we could throw a shoe or something."

The others laughed.

"Sorry," said Emily.

Laurie gave a small shiver. She turned to Leila, who shook her head with a smile and held up her wrists to show that she had no watch.

"Okay then," said Laurie. "You're right. Besides," she said darkly, "you know what would happen if we all lost our watches."

The others looked at her.

"If all our watches were gone," she said, drawing out the words, "everything would happen all at once."

But this they could not allow. "Laur-ie!" yelled Liam, and he started splashing her. The others joined in, relieved to break the tension that she was so expert at wrapping around them. Laurie dived in and skirting what she thought might be the center of the pond swam to the other side.

Finally Harriet said, "But we are forgetting the fish."

"Why don't you try again," fair-skinned Leila said to Liam. "And see who else is down there."

Liam walked back to the water nearest the rock with its burning candle. He bent down and swept his arms slowly from side to side, sieving the water through his fingers. He was jittery, all of a sudden, and hoped not to feel the slightest nibble.

The moon was up now, freed from the tree branches, though barely visible against the sky, which was shifting toward yellow.

"What?"

"It jumped into my hands. I didn't even try for it."

"What is it?"

"It's wiggling."

"Bring it over to the candle."

The fish was the size of an acorn squash but orange with yellow stripes from head to tail. Liam thought it looked more like a red snapper than a carp, but he thought that snapper did not live in sweet water. Fins and tail, too, were yellow. A strange dark eye, rimmed in black, looked at him unblinking. He didn't know what it was.

"Now what?" said Emily. "What do we do now?"

"Now we cook it," said Harriet. "Hurry and find sticks while there is still light."

"We'll need a knife," said Laurie. "Who's got one? There's something you do with a knife."

Liam held on to the fish and shook his head. He looked around at the others. Eli stood up again, clambered out of the water, and ran to his clothes, where he took a jackknife from his pocket. He offered it to his sister.

Laurie grabbed the knife from him. "Eli, where did you get that?" said Laurie. "Three-year-olds don't have knives."

Proud to have a big knife, Eli smiled and nodded. He had taken it from his father's desk.

"Getting the guts out of a fish is not easy," said Laurie. "If you do it wrong, it can make you sick. There are fish in Japan where you die right away if they don't get every speck of the liver out before you eat it. People fall backward off their counter stools in the restaurants. Poof. Like that. Nothing can revive them. I've seen pictures."

"I can do it," said Harriet. "I've gone fishing with my dad a lot. He showed me. It's a matter, he says, of slitting it *from its guggle to its zatch*. And scooping at the innards until they're all out."

"But do you kill it first?" asked Laurie.

"I forget," said Harriet.

Liam told them what had to be done. The life and death of fish were his intimate knowledge. They were what he knew. He took the fish to a farther rock and dashed it until it was still. He slit it open and gutted it. This night, in the summer before his eighth birthday, he was still a fisherman. He had decided a couple of years ago that he would eat no other animal until he was a teenager, and after that he would figure out what to do.

Liam brought the unusual golden fish back to the others and

rinsed it in the pond. The light had not yet gone from the day, and he could see the swirl of lifeblood in the water. Eli stood watching in silence while the others gathered sticks and branches and made a fire with Leila's matches in the nook of a few rocks.

Using Eli's knife, Liam whittled the ends of a forked stick. He jabbed the fish to skewer it, then held it over the fire. It grew heavier as it cooked. Soon he asked the others to spell him. Leila brought the candle over so they could see as it began to char and blacken.

Finally, when the fish was done, Liam put more branches under it to help lift it onto a bigger rock. The older children poked at it with their sticks.

"Come, Eli," Laurie said to her brother. "Come and have some dinner."

Little Eli approached the fish and looked at it. He shook his head.

"Don't you want some?" said Laurie.

With a voice like a bell, hesitant and sudden, Eli said, "No. It was beautiful. You made it ruined. I don't want some."

Eli left them and walked back to the bench. There he took off his underpants, still wet from the pond, and threw them into the forest. He got dressed, put on his shoes, tied the laces into knots, and walked away from the others. "You stupid sillyass," he hissed at himself.

"Hey, Eli," Laurie called after him. She didn't dare mention his talking. She wanted him to stay with them, and worried about his mood. "Don't you want your knife back?"

"You keep it," he called back. "I don't want it anymore."

He hurried off.

"Eli talked," Harriet said to Laurie.

"I know."

"Shouldn't we tell your parents?"

"My dad doesn't deserve to know," Laurie said. "But my mom has to know. She worries so much."

Liam stood beside the fish, master of it. He flaked some of it with a stick and picked at it with his fingers. "Needs something," he said. Harriet took some. "Salt?" she said. "Lemon?" She gave a small chunk of fish to Emily. Beside them, the pale girl, Leila, crouched on her haunches, watching but not eating.

"YOU STUPID STUPID boy," Eli kept repeating as he walked alone down the path. "What will you do now?" He was always careful to keep silent when people were around, except for occasional humming. But when he was alone, after checking that no one could overhear, he would utter all the words he had heard during the day—both the things they had tried to teach him and the ones they hoped he hadn't heard. Alone, he would also sing to himself, using words in the correct way, but never if anyone was near, anyone older than he was. With babies and cats, if the coast was clear, he would utter small things.

Laurie often tried with infinite sweetness and patience to teach Eli to speak. She considered it her job as his older sister. Sometimes she tried to teach him good words, like *elephant* and *truck* and *excellent,* but other times a look came over her and she would lower her voice to pronounce with special clarity *dickhead* and *Prozac* and *asshole.* Occasionally she would experiment and tell him the word for his small blue truck was really *swimming pool,* things like that, which he knew were wildly wrong, but he did not ask her why she was doing it. Of course, she was part of the reason he had decided not to talk in the first place. But only part of it. But now he, too, had ruined things.

Tricked into speech by the burnt and mangled fish, he was lost. He felt sick, useless. "You stupid," he wept. "You broke it. Now what will you do?"

AT THE POND, Harriet looked up. "What's that?"

"What?"

"In the bushes."

"Where?"

"Over there. I think it's watching us."

"Eli?"

"No, it's big. Much bigger. It breaks branches when it moves."

"Is it a bear?"

"I don't think so. I don't think there are bears here."

"A deer?"

"Deer would be scared of us."

"A man?"

"Listen . . . he's saying something."

"What?"

"Shh."

"I don't hear anything."

"Shut up, Harriet, it's because you're talking that we can't hear it."

"Well, I'm talking because I don't think there's anything there."

But the nothing in the woods seemed to grow into a bigger nothing, a darkness, and they all became afraid at the same moment that it was a man there, or a *something,* about to jump out of the woods and come for them.

Leaving their shoes and socks and clothes and leaving the

candle and the small cooking fire on the stones and the charred flakes of the once gold and yellow fish—still in their sodden underpants, bodies streaked with mud, lips blue, hair spiky and wet, shrieking and weeping—they ran down the path out of the shadowy forest and back to the grown-ups at their dinner party in the garden, which still held the last rays of light.

New wind currents eddied up from the ground as the children appeared, yelping like animals. Shivering and smeared with shadows of green and violet they called out.

"Mom, where are you?"

"Hey, Dad! There was something."

"We think there was something in the woods."

Then the organism that was the party inhaled and waved its claws and straightened and shook its appendages and stiffened around the long dining table and seemed to come apart, breaking up singly and severally into many private segments. The soft evening light glimmered on Philippa's gold bracelets and Olivia's silver hair ornament and Celia's emerald necklace and everyone's eyeglasses everywhere while the grown-ups rushed away from the table to gather and comfort their half-naked children.

"We heard something," panted Liam. "At the pond."

The other children agreed. They could not say exactly what it was that had frightened them.

"Well, it was sort of a thrashing about," Harriet said. "In the trees." Her hair was all heaved and matted on one side.

"Where's Eli? Was he with you?"

"Eli's fine. He left before us."

"Were you swimming?" asked Philippa. "Who was watching you?"

"Harriet and Laurie and the other girl."

"Harriet and Laurie are only ten. Anyway, let's go in and get you all washed up. What other girl?"

"Mom—"

"What is it, Laurie?" said Olivia, running toward her. "Where's Eli?"

"Mom. Eli talked. Words. Lots of them. Perfectly."

Olivia put her hand to her mouth as though to keep her own words inside. Then she said, "Where?"

"Up at the pond."

"No, I mean, where is he now?"

"Here someplace, he came back early."

"I think we should declare recess," Celia announced. "Until the little ones are calm and clean." She beckoned to Borsuk and told him to hold off on serving the dessert. "Pindar, my love," she said. "Would you blow out the candles? We'll light them again when we come back."

Pindar gave a quiet nod.

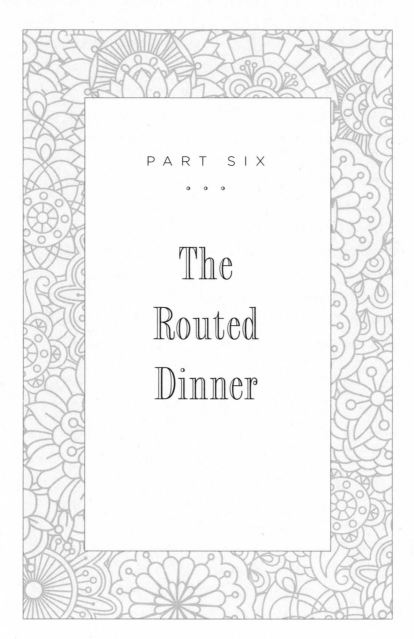

PART SIX

. . .

The
Routed
Dinner

Nathan Morrill shuddered at the confusion of young children, naked and damp and streaked with earth mold, all of them chattering. The wine, which had fizzed his brain at dinner, now bogged it down. He shuffled his feet along the grass as he walked, feeling old and lonely and childless. He missed having young children. Perhaps he had never had them. It seemed to him now as though his daughters, Philippa and Charlotte, had been born middle-aged. His new friend Leah, who had charmed him, had run off, perhaps to find the missing three-year-old boy. Too stiff with age and Lyme disease to follow her, he had lifted one of his heavy paws in benediction. "I'll wait for you," he called to her. "I'll be in the kitchen. Come and find me."

In the kitchen Borsuk was talking to Chhaya. His tuxedo, which no one had asked him to wear but no one had counseled against, since no one suspected he owned one, looked looser and less starched than it had at the beginning of the party, as though he had suddenly lost weight. It was an odd costume; it had certain turns of phrase—around the lapels and at the collar and cuffs—that spoke of a different century or continent. He stood facing Chhaya, who was wiping her hands on the dish towel hanging from her waist. Between them, on the kitchen table, sat an imposing confection covered with uncooked meringue. A handful of Fourth of July sparklers stood in a glass; they were to be inserted into the meringue once it came out of the oven. The fireworks had been Leah Cohen's idea, which she had proposed instead of ignited brandy on top. "You don't want to burn up good liquor," she had explained. "But you don't want to put cheap liquor on a grand dessert."

"She said to hold off," Borsuk told Chhaya.

"What hold off? I was just putting it into the oven."

"I'm glad I caught you," Borsuk said. "It is a disaster out there." He explained about the children running in from the forest. "That's them all going upstairs now, to wash. Complete mess. It will be an hour before they clean them up and find their clothes and get back to the table."

"But what am I to do? If she waits me too long, the ice cream inside will melt, and the cake underneath will get all wet, and the meringue, I don't know, it will blow down. All yesterday I made the cake and even I made the ice cream. Vanilla bean. Why do they break up my dinner party? It was going so well."

"It was going perfectly," Nathan Morrill agreed. "Your salmon was heavenly."

Chhaya's face contracted into a frightening mask. She ran out of the room.

Borsuk looked at Nathan Morrill and waved his hands in dismay.

"No," said Nathan. "Don't say that. I mean, don't gesture like that. We don't have time for gestures. Quick, find me a couple of bowls and a big spoon, a flat knife, and a spatula. What goes together can occasionally come happily apart. Put that bowl in the freezer. Watch."

Nat shuffled over to the sink and scrubbed as though preparing for surgery. The soap kept falling into the sink, as this was not a good time of day for his fingers. He flexed them under the hot water as though trying to melt them. As he rinsed and dried, he turned to Borsuk. "Look," he said, lifting his big flat hands with their thumbs lying alongside the palms. "These are not working too well tonight. Could you wash your hands and I'll talk you through it?"

Borsuk took off his tuxedo jacket, rolled up his sleeves, then washed. He tucked a dish towel into his collar and another one into his black cummerbund, and stood in front of the table. Following instructions, he scraped the covering of meringue off the ice cream and into the large bowl.

"Now," Nathan said. "The ice cream goes into the bowl we chilled in the freezer."

Borsuk sliced the ice cream off the top of the yellow cake and slid it into the bowl. It was as though he had been disassembling uncooked Baked Alaskas for years.

"Hurry. Meringue into the fridge, ice cream in the freezer, and all we need is a couple of small glasses of scotch whiskey."

Borsuk looked tentative about the drink.

"If anyone asks," Nathan said, "I'll say I made you do it. I will explain to them what we so brilliantly saved, and why we needed a bit of fortification at this point." He went to the cupboard and took down the bottle of scotch with both hands. Then he went to the baking drawer and took out the El Rey chocolate. "A bit of this goes very well with it. Oh, could you get the glasses? And pour?" He looked at his hands and shook them as though to get them working again. He held them to his ears, like a clock.

Borsuk looked puzzled.

"Joking," Nat said. "Sort of."

Olivia burst in. "Oh, I'm sorry," she said, looking around wildly. "Where is the cook? Has anybody seen little Eli? He's three, and doesn't talk. Or hardly. Did he come in here?"

Borsuk shook his head. "Only before dinner," he said. "Not since."

THERE WAS STILL a great scattering back and forth. Naomi and Sara ran up to the pond to get the clothing the children had left behind. They brought it all upstairs for the mothers to sort and distribute. The fathers had been sent downstairs, for there wasn't room for every parent to wash every child. Pindar and Celia walked with Stephen and Philippa in the garden, apologizing for the sudden interruption of festivities.

AS THOUGH BY prearrangement, Cameron and Naomi found each other at the far end of the driveway. "This can't happen," he said, kissing her.

"No," she said, letting herself fall against him. "I know."

"I mean, really it can't," he said.

"Even once? Just once?" she said.

"When?" he said.

"Now," she said, pulling away and taking his hand and leading him into the trees.

For a sweet fierce while the leaf mold of the forest floor was warm and fragrant and forgiving. Then there were two more who needed cleaning up. Naomi led Cam to the washroom in the garage.

SARA STOOD WITH Dennis by the statue. They were just far enough from her parents and the Barlows on the other side of the garden. They pretended they were talking about the statue, pointing at it from time to time.

"What happens now?" Dennis said.

"Well," said Sara. "The children get washed and we all go back to the table. . . ." But her voice was unsteady.

"You know that wasn't what I meant."

"I know. But I can't give you an answer just yet."

"I was going to ask you not to answer too quickly."

Naomi, who was gliding into the garden, came over to join them.

"Stand still," Sara told her, "while I groom you like a monkey. You have pieces of the forest in your hair." She plucked pine needles and bits of leaves. "Are you okay?"

"It's not as bad as it looks," said Naomi, smiling. She added, "A sweet and momentary fever."

Sara didn't know if Naomi was referring to her mood or her actions. She wanted to warn her about something, but who was she to talk? Perhaps for Naomi and Cam whatever had happened between them was encapsulated in the ritual time of this summer evening, perhaps for them the pain of loss would never come.

Naomi kissed her sister and thanked her, then ran off toward the house. Sara turned to Dennis. "How do I know"—she paused—"how do I know if the desire I feel right now is just the heat of the moment, or if it is something more terrible?"

"Terrible?"

"Terrifying, I mean."

"Do you think you are alone in this? Of course it is terrifying. The white heat of the soul. But about Africa, isn't it better to have something for a short time than not to have it at all?"

Sara gazed at him. The statue seemed to be smiling down at her.

JUST OUTSIDE THE library window a young bat hangs from the muscat grapes, then darts to the honeysuckle growing on the wooden trellis. Drunk with sweetness it loops through the air, back and forth.

Inside, in the dusk of the book-lined room, little Eli sleeps in a reading chair, folded up under a blanket.

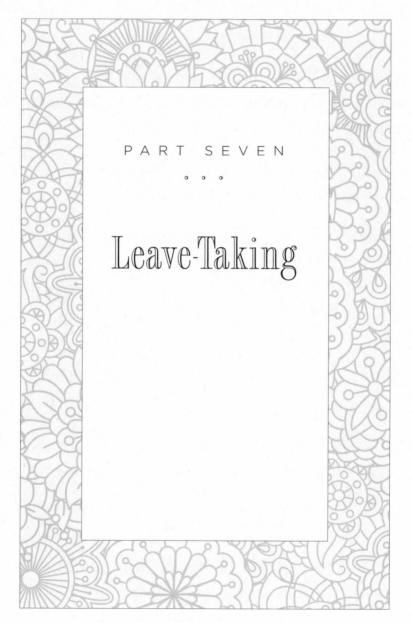

PART SEVEN

· · ·

Leave-Taking

The dinner party broke up just before dessert. The children, alarmed by the lateness of the hour or by some presence in the woods, had run screaming from the pond. The grown-ups fled from the table in the garden as though routed, and went to wash and calm their offspring. Leah Cohen chose that time to make her escape. She needed to take a stroll. If she hadn't gone off then, if she had been content to stay in the garden with Pindar and Celia and the older Barlows, then Adam and Eliza's church wedding would have taken place the next day instead of being postponed until September. Pindar and Celia would later wonder if Leah had realized this when she took off, but they could not believe that her actions had been intentional. Besides, she had always said that all long meals should have intermissions, in order to walk off what she called the stiffness of being.

Leah knew that the three-year-old Barlow boy was safely asleep in the leather reading chair in the library, wrapped in a paisley afghan, but she used the pretext of going to look for him as an excuse to walk up to the pond.

"Shall we come with you?" Sara offered. "Don't you want some company? It's about to get dark." Later she would regret not having insisted. She could have at least followed her grandmother from a distance. Even if she was still talking with Dennis. They could both have gone.

"No, no," said Leah. "You two should stay here and check the back of the garden." Sara and her young man were in some sort of turmoil. "Take some time, you two, to figure things out." Then, turning to Sara, "You know, my dear, it's absolutely no business of mine, but I really think you should do it, whatever it is that you are hesitating about. You should go. Otherwise you will always wonder about how it would have been. You will be left full of the regrets of failure to leap."

"Go? You mean to Africa?"

"Africa." Leah swept her arm to indicate the continent and all the distant world. "Africa. Greece. Everywhere. Look deeply, write about everything you see, and then, particularly, about what you fail to see. And remember to always shake out your boots in the morning."

"I will try," Sara said. She felt lighter, as though the decision had been made. She saw from the way Dennis shifted his head, ever so slightly, that he understood that she had decided to come to Africa with him.

"One more thing," Leah added, unable now to stop herself. "Be kind to each other. That is my remaining advice. Kindness is the only way you can see inside. *Ti esti philos? Allos ego.* What is a friend? Another self. That's the first thing you learn in Greek, but it could also be the last. And in the middle you learn *gnothi seauton*. Know thyself. Without knowing your own self, you can't know what 'another' self is. Your young man will teach you the Greek, but that is the least of it. Especially for you two. Give it time. Promise me that. Tonight isn't really your story—that will come after all this." Leah smiled at Sara and held out her arms for an embrace, for she was afraid she had said too much. She felt like a shepherd. One had to keep an eye on people. Leah kissed Sara, and then turned to Dennis and kissed him as well.

Leah was glad she knew where the little boy was, and knew that the others would find him before long. She felt incorrect running from the party, but her son, Pindar, would always do the same thing: He would escape his guests several times of an evening. "I felt I had to breathe," he would say later. Her daughter-in-law, Celia, tended to stay more in the thick of things, coping with what Pindar had left behind. Celia was good at that. Tonight, though, Leah was the one who needed some air. She pulled in a deep breath. It was almost dizzying how many people there were around the dinner table. A table full of desires. All those appetites. They seemed to be forming cobwebs that got in the way of her breathing.

The sky was now a dancing yellowish green, but the forest path led into darkness. The heat had not yet abated. Ferns brushed against Leah's dress as she peered into the woods; something moved in the fallen leaves. She was glad for that kind of company. She walked on, as if time pressed. Overhead, the gossamer of a web stretched between high branches caught an errant tangent of sunlight and glinted in the warm breeze. Not the single strand of the gypsy moth; more likely, she thought, a spider. The feverish air made familiar objects strange. As she walked, the rustling in the leaves persisted, as though some thing or being traveled beside her, tracing a line along the forest floor, its shudder braiding together the seen and unseen. A fox perhaps. Decades ago when she had owned this property there had always been a den or two behind the blackberries.

Leah had seen the children leave the table—there must have been five or six of them—during the asparagus course. Now, at the pond, she saw that they had made their own dinner. On the rock by the rushes a candle stood in a pool of wax, still burning. Beside it, charred sticks and a fish carcass, half-eaten, the rest blackened, skeleton askew. Probably carp. Fish was best for important dinners; red meat led to sluggish thoughts and vapid talk, the guests lethargic, senses dulled, eyes bland. But with the eating of fish, new connections sparked everywhere, electric.

The dinner in the garden was meant to celebrate her grandson Adam's wedding. It was the "rehearsal dinner," though everyone had been refusing to call it that, as though the term were somehow bad luck. So it was to celebrate the wedding, but it had also, she knew, been performative. Finally. At table, under cover of broad daylight, well, of early midsummer evening daylight, and in full company, Adam and his bride, Eliza, had eloped. Leah had been the only witness. The only witness aside from Harry, but he was the celebrant.

Weddings, with their sewing together of the older generations, always seemed to open up something as well, revealing an uncanny cleft in time, and Leah could suddenly feel the presence of her dead, of friends long gone. Her mind felt split, as though she were swinging between now and then.

Of course, it had been salmon, too, at a party Leah had given in Paris many decades earlier when she was a very young woman, back when love was new and fierce and so often connected with violence and wine. Of her friends at that party, all were now dead except for her husband. She and Gabriel had never been formally divorced or legally separated, but except for the rare times every decade or so when they would happily reconvene, they lived as though sweetly divorced. None of their friends could understand why they both preferred this ambiguous situation. They were not together, yet Leah knew, and Gabriel agreed, that they each felt somehow bound to the other. At least this way, she thought, they never chafed, never tired of each other, though there were times when she would have welcomed taking those risks. If Leah had ever wanted to marry someone else, she would have requested, and he would have given, his blessing.

Gabriel was living in France. He had sent a sweet note regretting that he could not be present at the wedding. He was alive, but all those others were gone. Where was the museum of her dead? She had never said goodbye to them, to Murray, for example, who was old even then and sodden with absinthe. Murray, who started museums all over France and said his museums were like caviar—fish eggs, he meant—because so many were spawned but few survived. Leah had not said goodbye to Oliver and his Olga, who assaulted each other at dinner parties and sometimes had to be separated and bandaged after the soup course. She had not said goodbye to Clara, who used the truth as a scimitar; or to Céline, who was "so pretty she didn't have to know how to read," as Clara had said. Even to Pierre, her charming and suffocating lover during that time, Leah had not said goodbye. That dinner in Paris was also in a garden, also on a summer night. It was between the two wars, although one didn't know that then.

But on this night in 1991, here in Brookline, Leah was glad for the interruption of the children forcing the recess in the dinner, allowing her to walk to her ancient pond. She needed these moments alone, partly because she had been so taken with, so intoxicated by, her dinner partner. She had thought that she and the century were too far gone to be capsized like this. She had thought she was unenchantable.

When Leah had lived on this property she had shaped the

gardens, cleared the pond. She had dug the water lilies into the muck and planted the scarlet cardinal flowers to exclaim among the rushes.

And now, partly because the pond had once been hers, and partly because she was both old enough and still young enough to do what she wanted, she took off her mauve silk dress and walked toward the water in her slip. No one would see her. Everyone down at the house was rushing about—all those agitated children with chattering teeth and stories of frights in the woods.

How close the water felt to air—that warm black surface reflecting the yellow-green of the sky. Under her feet, mud soft as kisses. Nearby something roiled the surface. A fish brushed against her legs, then came back and nudged her, as though pushing her away from the edge.

Was it too odd for a woman in her early nineties to be wading alone in a pond, under the black of the pine trees and the clear chartreuse of the evening air? It was her pond, or had been once. And on this evening her pond was one of those hinges of being, letting her swim back through her past, back to bathing as a girl in England. All those sun-splashed river outings around Oxford with her older brother and his friends. Then, later, with her own friends. Her parents tried to forbid such expeditions, protesting that she was too young and her companions unsavory. Leah disobeyed and went anyway. Later still, after she had been exiled to Paris and was living on her own, there were trips to the outlying forests at Fontainebleau and Rambouillet with daylong picnics in the dappled shade, gatherings that always engendered more yearnings than there were people to go around. At sunset she and her companions would migrate through the woods to one of the ponds, where they would swim far into the night.

Surely Leah must have led some sort of existence between the watery places of her life, but thinking back this evening, her entire history seemed collapsed into a succession of lakes, rivers, oceans. Perhaps she had been a water creature in a former life: a speckled trout, a dolphin. When she and Gabriel and five-year-old Pindar fled from France to America in the mid-1930s, she discovered the great sand beaches of New England. She introduced them to her son and then to his two sisters born in America, who never loved the water or their mother as much as he did. As Gabriel traveled more and came home less, there were fewer excursions north to Crane's Beach (as it was known then) or south to Horseneck or the Cape. Finally, when Gabriel seemed to have settled in Europe without them, Leah's life with her children became centered around this house in Brookline and its small pond, this old pond where she was floating now, on her back, looking up at the sky, floating and being prodded by some sort of snout. She splashed, floundered, gulped water. Then she saw the distinctive fin and smiled.

The immense carp had first appeared in the pond in the 1940s. She had fed him in the old days, bread scraps mostly, and had always fancied that he knew who she was. He had seemed ancient even then, with his long feelers and the half-moon-shaped bites taken out of his tail fin. She saw that fin now, unmistakable as he flicked it above the surface. She lunged for him and he seemed to allow her to hold him for a moment or two, before he twisted and was gone.

Leah spiraled out to where the waterweeds would not reach her. Away from the shallows, springs bubbled up and the water had a velvety feel, making her want to float just under the surface.

Attack. Something gripped her from within, gorging her with pain. She tried to move her arms but succeeded only in flipping over, facedown. As she tilted her head back to breathe she felt the muscular body of the carp nudging her higher in the water so she could take a breath. He was trying to save her like the ancient Greek dolphin saved the lyre player Arion. She was in too much pain to thank him.

"LEAH! IS THAT you?" Celia Cohen made a heavy leap into the water. Weighted down by her dress, her shoes, she stroked clumsily to the middle of the pond.

The carp swam away as Celia clutched Leah's chest and wrenched her around. The two women flailed in the dusk. Much the taller, Leah coughed and clawed, then tried get on top of Celia, to step on her and hold her down, to stop the pain.

Celia, grappling with her mother-in-law's surprising strength, gulped water, sputtered. "Let go, Leah. It's me. I'm saving you."

Leah twisted her head around to see, her long face looming with terror and incomprehension. She scratched at Celia's eyes.

"Off me," Leah said, eloquent for a moment, majestic. "I am looking for something." She spat and tried to roll over. But Celia acted as though she hadn't heard and pinioned Leah's arm behind her. "Ow," Leah grunted. "That's my arm."

Darkness after.

Voices. Voices through the watery dark:

"Le . . . ah."

"Are you walking?"

"Only if the S omnibus has stopped."

"Oh, it's long gone."

"I have to get to Gare Saint-Lazare; I live on the Right Bank."

"Why on earth go home? Come and see my place; I'm right near Denfert."

"Leah?"

"Leah, Leah! Is that you? It's getting so late. I have to say good night."

Leah recognizes old Murray emerging from the shadows with his ancient undulating gait. She is standing at the edge of the garden of the little stone house she rented in Paris in the mid-1920s. She is young. It is the end of her dinner party, the one where she lost a fox and found a husband.

Old Murray weaves toward Leah. Always more formal than anyone else, he is wearing tails of an ancient scalloped cut, his bow tie askew with the lateness of the evening. He purses his lips and kisses her, tickling her face with his drooping mustache that looks a bit greenish in the dim light. "Thank you so much," he murmurs. "Your salmon was superb. Everything."

"Goodbye, Murray," Leah says, backing off a bit, for his breath smells of swamp. "Stay well. You didn't think the fish was too dry?"

Up above, the lingering twilight of Paris in midsummer has given way to night, saying, *Here, you take over,* and the immense hinged dome of darkness is speckled with stars. All of Leah's other guests—full of strange and sudden energy—are roaming the limestone terrace and the garden; under the trees they catch each other and embrace, holding on a moment too long, then reaching for a hand, a waist, a breast. No one wants to spin apart now into separate elements. This is when things get said that wouldn't otherwise because the hour is so late. Censors are off. Secrets blurt themselves. Explanations filigree into narratives, stories compress themselves into a handful of syllables.

Beside the fountain, Olga confides about Oliver, "I slashed canvas, arm. He held my throat, strangled me. I'd no voice for days."

Leah's own arm aches at these words; her throat constricts as though someone is holding her too tightly.

A man's voice, behind the trees, can barely be heard as he summarizes, "But it was not his. Nature came to her rescue. He was not to know."

Although Leah has not meant to neglect her other guests, all evening she has given her attention to dark-eyed Gabriel Cohen. After drinking wine under the chestnut tree they walk through the garden naming flowers, listening for night birds; finally she sits by his side at one of the tables on the terrace. They talk and listen as though already interlocked.

Why have they never met before? Gabriel, a scholar of classical languages, has always lived in Paris; Leah has been here now for five years, sent from England when she was twenty by her parents, who were bewildered by her behavior and shocked by her paintings. From the family lawyer in Oxford, Leah receives a generous allowance—as long as she consents to stay in France. Her parents come and visit from time to time.

Gabriel and Leah, for five years, these two souls wandering through Paris, always with the negative coincidence of just missing each other: Several times they have been in the same cafés, at the same gatherings, for though Gabriel is a scholar he prefers to spend his time with artists. For a while Gabriel and Leah each had an affair, unbeknownst, with the same dancer, a Parisian woman as mysterious and discreet as she was unfaithful. Perhaps they glimpsed each other after all, but only just. Perhaps Gabriel's reflection lingered a moment in the mirror one afternoon when he was just leaving, and Leah just joining, their shared lover. But their meeting never locked into focus as it finally has on this summer evening in the mid-1920s in Montparnasse.

The women scatter now, looking for handbags and feather boas and tasseled shawls; brief flares and pools of light appear as the men strike matches for a last pipe or cigarette.

Everyone else is standing, ready to say their terrible goodbyes, but Gabriel remains seated, his hand stroking the stained tablecloth toward Leah, who sits beside him. She is chattering to keep her guests from noticing the hour, for parties can collapse, everyone deciding at the same instant that it is time to go, as when at the opera the applause dies all at once, or like those animal species who spring apart after mating with neither tenderness nor regret.

It is in the ending of the party, Leah knows, that we can see the whole thing: what has gone on as well as what failed to happen, what was served up, what ignored, all the delights, gaffes, torments. What glories! Hopes! Desperations! Of course, the extremely late hour can also bring strange urges—for folly, substance, change.

Then, too, there are those special demons who hover at the ends of parties, come to make mischief. Some are simply the demons of fatigue: *Let us flee!* they whisper in your ear. *Say anything, say whatever you must, but get us out of here.* Stronger, deeper, though, than any fatigue or fear is the grief of leave-taking, full of its own compulsions.

"Leah!" Oliver interrupts.

Leah inhales, coughs, puts a hand on the table to steady herself, notices how small the space is between her own hand and Gabriel's. She is drunk with him. She knows the signs: mind on edge, soul stung, the piracy of longing. Smiling, she stretches out her legs and finally stands up.

"Leah, angel," Oliver says. "Your soup was tart and green as English virgins and your garden is an invitation. The roses alone are enough to drive one to folly. *Cuisse de nymphe . . . cuisse de nymphe . . .* well, exactly." As he kisses her, he smells of tobacco and turpentine and stale sex. "I'm so sorry about the broken windowpanes and all the wineglasses. I'll send my ancient carpenter in the morning. I'm embarrassed about my matches. I've ruined your tablecloth. I'm so clumsy with my arm like this. What a damnation." Like some ungainly bird he flaps his bandaged arm in its sling. "Such a lovely cloth it was."

"No, really," Leah says, her own arm aching as she looks at his. "It doesn't matter. Not at all! It was a rag from the flea market." She looks beyond him into the shadows, where other guests appear as though floating in the pools of darkness between the garden candles.

"I will take you to buy a new cloth. We will go searching. And then we will have lunch. Yes?"

For a moment Leah despises Oliver for not being Gabriel, whose every offer she yearns for. She assumes it is Olga who has wounded Oliver's arm, but his love affairs are many and convoluted, often tangled with obscure violence. "Lunch?" she says to him. "No one will mind?" Suddenly bitter, she realizes that she herself will mind: To spend her breath with anyone but Gabriel will lead to suffocation. Thinking of it she can hardly inhale, wants to free herself from such a rendezvous. But what she wants is decoupled from what she can say, and she sees herself about to accept Oliver's invitation. Perhaps it is the wine that is making things waver so. The world feels billowy, the pull of gravity distorted, as though the earth's rotation has taken on a wobble. Though buoyant, she feels uncertain and may stumble into the laps of the wrong gods.

Oliver smiles, strokes Leah's black hair with his good hand. "Mind?" he replies. "They are all too busy." He smiles as though pleased that he does not have to hide or explain the other women in his life to her. "They are minding one another." Then he embraces her; it is awkward, with his bandaged arm up in the air. "When shall we do it?" he asks. "When shall we do that thing?" There was a time when Leah would have done anything with Oliver, but now, even with only one of his arms around her, the hug is too constricting and she pulls away from him, gasping.

"Good night, Leah darling," says Olga, whose pale expanse of bosom is framed by her black fringed shawl and by the purple boa she has kept around her neck all evening, barely hiding her bruises.

Leah embraces Olga, with her scent of patchouli.

"The salmon?" says Olga. "Not at all dry; your fish was distinguished and your meringues with wild berries . . ."

Old Murray navigates through the darkness to join them. "Olga," he says. "There you are. I couldn't leave until I found you, but I no longer see so well in the dark." He nibbles at the ends of his drooping whiskers, then says, "You will let me visit you tomorrow? If I don't see you, I will flood with melancholy."

Olga takes Murray's arm and walks off with him.

These people are so old, twenty-five-year-old Leah thinks.

They cannot still, at their age, be feeling what they claim to feel. They are simply playacting gallantry.

Now Gabriel's mistress comes to the table. Leah and Gabriel sway imperceptibly from each other. Gabriel asks with studied patience, "Céline, darling, what is it?"

"I can't find my purse."

"How do you women lose these things?" he says. Then, relenting, "What does it look like?"

"Red. With a strap." Céline pouts, flicks her head back, a posture that is no longer beguiling.

"Red?" he says, as though the color is new to him and incomprehensible.

"It's the one I always have. You know what it looks like."

Gabriel gives a subtle kick, nudges something under the table. Leah feels this, wonders if it is Céline's purse, and realizes that she is blushing. She tells herself he might have been kicking a cat or a stone.

"*Chérie,*" Gabriel says, brighter now. "Did you leave it in the house?"

As Céline hurries away into the molten darkness, Gabriel turns to Leah, who sways toward him again. "So lovely." *You,* he means, but shyness makes him add, "The evening."

Leah asks him, "Do you really have to be off? Won't you stay? I've hardly gazed at you." Her voice has a breathless desperation she has never heard before. She can hardly talk.

But now Leah's lover, Pierre, hurries by, chasing Leah's fox, which has escaped from the house. Leah found the fox half dead in a trap, when she was on a spring walking trip in the forests of southern France. It was a time when she was half-feral herself: The end of a love affair had left her unable to paint or to sit in company with others. She had lost all desire and to be around anyone at all felt like touching a new burn. Her soul had shriveled to the size of an olive pit. All she could do was take long walks, not because she wanted to, but because she could not stand to be indoors.

The fox had tried to savage Leah when she freed him from the trap, but she wrapped him up in her canvas coat so he couldn't attack her and took him home in order to nurse his leg. At first they sat up nights; together they refused to eat. He spurned her but tried to snatch wine from her glass. She pushed him away. Sleepless, they snarled at each other, swore in their own tongues, his vocabulary—screams and growls and sharp ratcheting fox calls—much more varied than her own. Over time, however, they both took to eating again. The fox grew used to her, allowing closeness and caresses, though his hind leg never completely recovered from being smashed by the trap and he ran with a syncopated gait. One day, when Leah found him licking curiously at a dried puddle of linseed oil, she remembered her own taste for painting as well.

Running among the guests on the terrace, Pierre finally catches the fox and drapes it over his shoulder. This is new, for the animal has always been skittish with anyone but Leah, and Pierre has always complained that its musky scent was too close to that of skunk. Pierre now leans toward Leah, cupping her chin in his hand, saying softly, "You must let them go now, your guests. They have to get home. It has gotten late. Time to sleep."

Leah tries to pull away from his grip. "Sleep!" she exclaims. "I couldn't possibly. Look up at that sky: too much throbbing up there ever to sleep." She points toward the heavens but her arm swings wildly. "What a voluptuous clangor," she tries to say. She is dwelling on her consonants, for vowels have become like bubbles. "What about a swallow of cognac? A finger of scotch?" She wishes Pierre would crawl off somewhere to sleep, but he stands there, watching her, the fox on his shoulder.

Gabriel glances at the house and turns back to Leah. "You're right: The night is very full," he says. "It deserves notice." Then, seeing the older couple who have still not left, he gets up. "Goodbye, Murray. Good night, Olga." Handshakes and watery sounds of kisses.

Leah is puzzled, for she thought that Olga and Murray left hours earlier. She wonders exactly how many layers of scarves and shawls Olga is wearing to hide her bruises. How does Oliver cause such violence? This is not the first time he has provoked one of his women. Isn't Olga too old to slash canvases and men? Leah tries to imagine a knife in Olga's pudgy hands—palette knife? Fish knife? When does it stop, she wonders, the vehemence of love?

Olga touches Leah's face. "Such young skin," she says. Then she grabs a handful of Leah's hair. "This mane of yours. You look like a mermaid. You are too young to color this yet, I think."

Leah does not like Olga's fetid breath and wants to get away, but one of Olga's elaborate finger rings has snagged in her hair and she must wait while Olga disentangles herself, muttering, "So black, so black," then calling out, "Clara! Has Leah sat for you? Have you painted this siren?"

"She won't let me," a voice calls back, laughing. "I ask her every time I see her."

"Oh, Leah! Shame!" says Olga. "Are you so shy? Everyone has painted *me* at one time or another."

Leah flings up her hands in a little shimmying dance, twisting free of Olga's grasp. A painter herself, she knows the power of gaze and prefers to be on the observing end of it. She is not shy, exactly, but does not want her body held captive in the plane.

Gabriel and Leah sit down again. Pierre stands a little distance away, watching her with Gabriel, as he has all evening. Leah wishes he would stop lurking. "I thought they had already left, Murray and Olga. Several times, even," she says. "It must be the Bordeaux." She raises her eyes toward Pierre and the animal. "It is pure folly for me to keep that fox in the city. But I would hate to let him go. He shares my table. . . ."

"That's not all he shares," a woman's voice calls out from the garden.

Leah looks up. Turning to Gabriel she says softly, "Before tonight, he has never attacked anybody, at least not since his very first days with me when he was miserable and wild. Since then, never."

"Well," says Gabriel. "Perhaps no one else tries to tease him by dangling pieces of cheese as bait."

This is not where Leah wants the conversation to go. But with Pierre there listening to them, she cannot figure out what she needs to say. Instead she points to the russet fox, who has woken up and is following the conversation with its yellow eyes, tall ears pointed forward, black nose quivering. "He always knows when I am talking about him," Leah says. "He wakes up at three in the morning," she continues. "He howls, carving out new tributaries of alarm in my veins. Throws me out of bed. We slip downstairs. I let him out, but he doesn't want that and he just sits yelping on the doorstep." She pauses again.

"Every night?"

"Many nights," Leah says. "We stay in the kitchen. He calms down if there is something good to eat. He likes strawberries.

Apple tart. If there is nothing sweet, we both stay awake and vigilant: We sit at table together and shudder till dawn."

Pierre looks uncomfortable at these confessions; he approaches, putting a proprietary hand on Leah's shoulder. "Did you have a good time at your party?"

Leah flinches. There's something she has to say and if she can't find it, can't call it out, she will gutter like a candle. If she does say it, though, Pierre will tear her to pieces. Already his hand is gripping her shoulder bones too tightly, twisting her spine, crushing her lungs. All Leah can think to say is "I still am."

Wait, she thinks. *That is not it. Stay.* The evening is slipping through her grasp. Time is opening up like the chestnut tree above her into endless branchings, then budding into leaf, exploding into the white panicles of its flowers, then coalescing again, folding in, washing over her like waves.

The fox chooses this moment to leap down from Pierre's shoulder and run off toward the garden. When Pierre chases after it, Leah touches Gabriel's hand, then draws back. "Is it true?" she asks him. She does not know yet what she is asking. In the thrill of nearness her temples throb.

Before Gabriel can answer, Clara dashes up to them, her white shirt flamboyant in the darkness. "Oh, Leah. Leah. I am so sorry. I've done it again."

"What is it? What have you done?"

"I've ruined your dinner party. No wonder no one invites me."

"But, Clara, everybody invites you. Look: Here you are!" Leah stands up and throws both her hands out to indicate the garden, space, being. "Let me see that poor arm." She draws

Clara's arm toward her, pulls up the flowing sleeve, and lifts the bandage. She winces. For a moment she can't speak. She shakes her head. "It makes my own arm hurt just to look at it. I can't think of what got into him. It's my fault: I should never have brought him down to dinner. I am such a fool."

"No, no," says Clara. "You mustn't blame the fox. I was teasing him with Camembert. I wanted to see if he would jump."

"I will take you to my doctor in the morning."

"Oh, no, really," Clara says. "I barely feel it. Besides, I ruined your party. Daniel and Louisa left before we sat down to eat. I don't even know how I managed to upset them. I thought everybody knew. All I said was that she looked beautiful and not at all pale, considering." Clara hesitates. "How could she have kept such a thing from her husband? How on earth do people lose track of each other? Do you think I should stick to the weather? God, hasn't it been glorious these past few days? Look what the sun has done to Gabriel—all the dark gone from under his eyes—and you, Leah, you look all startled and radiant as though you had just invented something like moonlight or love."

Adopting a broad sweet smile, a desperate foolish innocence, Leah gambles, "Clara. What about a cognac?"

"Oh no, I couldn't possibly stay," says Clara. "It's gotten so late. I'm deluged with sleepiness. Good night, Leah. Thank you so much." Then, turning to Gabriel, "Watch your step here, Gabriel," she adds. "More men have swooned in this garden than anywhere else in Paris. You're just the type to be totally defenseless against Leah's charms. . . . She'll probably ask you to teach her something, to give her lessons, and she will be serious. That's the trouble."

"Oh," laughs Gabriel. "I'd love to, but no danger there, I'm afraid. What would a painter want with old languages? What would a painter want with Greek?"

"Well, you watch out for her. Leah's immensely clever. And you can never tell whether she prefers men or foxes or absolutely no one at all. Good night, Gabriel." Noisy kisses. "Good night, Leah. Good night, Pierre."

Pierre approaches when she calls to him, and Clara blows him a kiss, careful to keep her distance from the fox. "Come, Clara," he says. "I'll walk you out." He meanders with Clara to the gate; the fox crouches on his shoulder, the white tip of his tail flicking back and forth.

Gabriel turns to Leah. "Could we go into the kitchen and steal a glass of water? A wild thirst has come." His hand feathers her back, then rests there.

"Come," Leah says, taking his arm. Then at the kitchen door she stops. "Greek," she says.

"What?"

"Afterward, Hebrew, but first Greek. Clara was right, that I would ask you for lessons."

Gabriel drops his voice. "But how will you have time? First you have Pierre, then you seem to have Oliver. Oliver will probably strangle you if you study with me."

"Forget them both," Leah says. "We have all the time in the world."

"When?" he asks, the single syllable like a gong.

"Tomorrow," she says, pulling on the vowels to keep them from burbling. With her head tilted back Leah looks up into the chestnut tree and the Parisian night sky above.

"When," Gabriel says again.

"Noon. Café du Dôme."

"Consider it done," he says. "We are already there."

Leah and Gabriel stand together just outside the house, watching as his ex-mistress Céline makes her way toward the empty table with its scarred cloth where they were sitting. She kneels down to dive underneath for the red purse.

In an instant Leah sees that she will run off with Gabriel, leaving the fox with Pierre. Gabriel will give her lessons, he will give her children, they will marry. Suddenly the evening flutters madly, billowing like a length of white linen, slipping through Leah's grasp. She wants to press it into limestone, anchor it there, among the whorls and helices of fossils tunneling through the stones of the terrace and the walls of the house itself. There, in the candlelight by the kitchen door, standing with Gabriel, her fingers just touching his, she can see a skeleton of sorts, embedded in the stone of the doorframe, some ancient fish, spine and head and eye and ribs and fins, captured and pressed into the ancient limestone.

More voices:

"Has the last metro gone?"

"What about the all-night 'bus'?"

"Is anybody going toward Père Lachaise?"

"Champs-Elysées?"

"Have some," a man's voice says, very close to her. "This is for you."

Then it is dark again.

NOW, IN HER old pond in Brookline, Leah stopped pulling at the arm that was dragging her across the water. She needed all the strength of these last moments to watch the ending of the day that had escaped the colors of the earth to a hue far beyond emerald. The nearer heavens grew darker and yet more luminous, for light was no longer separated from shadow and night was no longer separated from day. Time had ceased quivering and coiling back on itself. It had become taut and resonant and she was enfolded in its infinite smoothness.

All the birds of dusk now burst into song and noises come from every rock and tree and fern as though the thoughts of each thing, living or not, can suddenly be heard. The songs call space into existence and give it shape. Here exists. And here. It is what it is. At this moment. Now.

ACKNOWLEDGMENTS

o o o

Work on this novel has been going on for as long as the millennium. It is a joy—finally—to thank friends and family for their inspiration and guidance.

Barry Mazur, the late Zeke Mazur, Sasha Makarova, and Naia Zostriana Mazur have always acted as igniters of soul fire and helped me with the conflagrations that followed. Zeke Mazur, although he claimed not to be a reader of fiction, gave a generous and close reading of a late draft, making comments on almost every page, saving me from numerous missteps and follies, and pointing out felicities I had not seen.

Elizabeth Dane, Dustin Beall Smith, Jamaica Kincaid, Sue Trupin, Susan Holmes, Persi Diaconis, Elaine Scarry, Philip Fisher, Michel Chaouli, Jane Hirshfield, Eva Brann, Cecie Dry, Paul Dry, Joyce Olin, Chris Nelson, Milen Poenaru, Valentin Poenaru, Dorina Papaliou, Apostolos Doxiadis, Nan Cuba, Alison Moore, Marta Maretich, Michael Alford, Ed Howe, Kim Keown, Ellen Kaplan, and Robert Kaplan have long influenced and inspired me by their lives and their works and their astonishing gardens. Discussions with all the members of the Brann/

Kutler Seminars at St. John's College over the past fifteen years have been crucially important.

Conversations in beautiful and otherworldly settings with Margaret Hearst, Will Hearst, Jennifer Saffo, Paul Saffo, Mary Lee Coffey, Shelby Coffey, Stacey Hadash, Terry McDonell, Danny Hillis, Russell Chatham, and the late Jim Harrison have been wonderfully provocative and catalytic. I'm grateful to the Hearsts for bringing these conversations about.

I've long been blessed by the warm companionship and wise counsel of the late Alexandra Dor-Ner, the late Zvi Dor-Ner, Tamar Dor-Ner, Dan Krockmalnic, Daphne Dor-Ner, Aaron Kammerer, Win Lenihan, Anna Lenihan, Vida Kazemi, Paul Horowitz, Melissa Franklin, Sarah Kafatou, and the late Fotis Kafatos. My thanks to them for their constancy.

Thanks, also, to my faculty colleagues, fellow alumni, and students at the MFA Program for Writers at Warren Wilson for their intense listening to early drafts of these chapters.

I am immensely grateful to Andrea Walker at Random House for her editorial vision, brilliance, and generosity. Every interaction with her has brought joy during a difficult time. Many thanks to Janet Wygal and her team of copy editors, whose edits have been meticulous and pleasing.

I am wildly lucky to have Esmond Harmsworth as my agent. His intellect, generosity, fearlessness, and patience are astonishing.

But most of all, my thanks to Barry, who endows the world with light, and my life with passion.

ABOUT THE AUTHOR

GRACE DANE MAZUR is the author of *Hinges: Meditations on the Portals of the Imagination; Trespass: A Novel;* and *Silk: Stories.* She was deep in postdoctoral research on morphogenesis in silkworms when she left biology completely in order to write fiction. Most recently, she has been on the fiction faculty at Harvard Extension School and at the MFA Program for Writers at Warren Wilson College. A native of Brookline, she lives in Cambridge and Westport, Massachusetts, with her husband, the mathematician Barry Mazur.

gracedanemazur.org

ABOUT THE TYPE

This book was set in Sabon, a typeface designed by the well-known German typographer Jan Tschichold (1902–74). Sabon's design is based upon the original letterforms of sixteenth-century French type designer Claude Garamond and was created specifically to be used for three sources: foundry type for hand composition, Linotype, and Monotype. Tschichold named his typeface for the famous Frankfurt typefounder Jacques Sabon (c. 1520–80).